_Thanks
Rob_

Five Days
To A
Security
Breakdown!

Five Days To A Security Breakdown!

Leadership, Management, SPAM, ROI, Identity theft, Outsourcing, Downtime, Business Foundations, Trust, Integrity and Value.

You didn't ask for it but you're getting e-mails about mortgage rates, finding your true love, increasing your body length

or starting a business with an Asian prince.

Author **Rick Smith**

Introduction by **Shane Pitman**

ISBN 1-58961-239-6

Published by PageFree Publishing, Inc.
733 Howard Street
Otsego, MI 49078
www.pagefreepublishing.com

Dedication

I would like to dedicate this book to my parents who instilled in me the belief that I could do anything.

Introduction

Dear Reader,

It has been my distinct pleasure to work with Rick Smith over the past years and to experience, first hand, his ability to not only understand the technology required to implement a safe and secure system, but more importantly his innate ability to separate the technical from the non-technical issues. This unique ability, coupled with his extensive business experience, provides readers with an insight into areas and practices that they might never have thought of as a threat to their personal security or the security of their business.

When Rick first mentioned his thoughts on creating a series of publications (ID10T Errors) and writing a book, I knew he would be successful. Now that I have read the book, I am even more convinced. While extremely funny, the lessons that can be learned from these stories are very real as are the risks and consequences that can occur when these types of issues are ignored. Technology and the advancements being made are remarkable, but even the most advanced security technology is worthless if we don't secure the weakest link, the people we entrust and employ.

Luckily for me, I had the privilege of experiencing Rick's expertise first hand. Through this book, you can get close glimpse of what it's like.

This book can save you time and money. It will make you laugh. Read it and pay attention. I'm glad I did and I look forward to the next ID10T Errors publication.

Take Care,

Shane Pitman

Foreword

"400 percent increase in "Hacker" attacks in the first half of the year!"

"Be aware of a new & very dangerous technique, known as `spoofing,` that could trick Web surfers into handing over critical data and financial information to imposters."

"New dangers arise as Open-source model seems to be a magnet for attackers."

"The U.S. Securities and Exchange Commission and the Department of Justice filed charges on Thursday against a 19-year-old Pennsylvania man accused of using a Trojan horse program to steal money from another man's brokerage account."

"That hacker is no longer just the kid next door with an intense curiosity about the nature of our surroundings. He's not alone anymore and there's a change in the air...credit card fraud, identity theft, corporate espionage, rogue nations and terriost groups preparing for cyber warfare; the elements of fraud and worse seem to have overtaken the general urge to commit vandalism."

"Can Spam. Is that really how we refer to important legislation that is supposed to be help establish a framework of technological, administrative civil and criminal tools? Unfortunately this is potentially just another Anti-spam bill, which are normally written poorly and unconstitutionally overbroad. The things people write just to get you to buy the story or re-elect them are truly amazing. After all wasn't it a politician that created the Internet?"

These are scary headlines. It is true the volume of these types of activities is increasing, the complexity is increasing, and therefore, the associated risks and costs are increasing. It would seem that until there are some sorts of global agreements that any attempts to find legislation as a solution are going to be unenforceable.

The good news:

1. Manufacturers will put out better hardware and software.
2. We will all continue to change the way we live and conduct business.
3. We will all learn how to protect ourselves against the risks and costs.

The fundamental security question facing us all today is how to allow everyone access to more information and services, while not compromising our own freedom and security. Security is about the environment, the processes and the policies involved. Individuals and corporations will eventually find the right balance. This book offers you help in finding that balance and will save you time getting there.

Preface

This book is written in the standard format for the ID10T Errors series of publications. It's written to make you smile and to make you think. Each chapter presents a fictional story or stories with issues and situations that we all face from time to time. At the end of each chapter there is an ID10T Errors section in which we offer suggestions and solutions. I'm sure you will see similarities with your own real life experiences and our stories.

In this particular book there are five chapters. They are named for the days of the week. Each day a different staff member from our company offers a perspective of the day's issues and events. There are many reasons, other than the sheer entertainment value, that could cause one to choose to read this book. The solutions that the author offers to the technological and human issues raised in this story bring great value to this publication. Properly implemented, any one of these solutions could offer you a value that far exceeds the cost of this publication. The benefits that could be reached through the use of just one of the solutions offered in this book could potentially last for years to come.

I would like to offer the disclaimers as follows:

1. All of the stories, situations and characters in this book are completely fictional. Any resemblance to anyone or any situation is strictly by accident and not intentional. During the 25 years of

professional experiences and lord knows how many years of personal experiences I never knew of situations and/or people exactly like any in this book. Chill out. It's not you... you're unique.

The descriptions of people and/or projects in this book are to add color and should not be viewed as politically correct communication for your next corporate meeting. This kind of stuff will get you in trouble.

- Trust me, I would never look at one of our sales staff who is experiencing a drop in his personal sales and ask, "Are you finding it difficult to look back at your past job experiences and find any help other than `would you like fries with that?."

My basic approach to security, systems, processes, procedures and technology:

Do you remember when seat belts first came out? Weren't they a pain in the ass? Everyone we know wanted to take them out of their car. Eventually we learned to simply get in our cars and buckle up. Today that simple process occurs for most of us every time we get in our car and we don't even think about it. Security isn't just about hardware and software. It's also about changing the processes and procedures for all of us. We all must change the way we live and the way we conduct business. We must constantly keep talking and measuring our efforts so that we might succeed. The best advice might be "Get in the car, buckle up, obey the rules of the road and use your common sense." Come on let's go for a ride.

Monday

Hello. My name is Craig and I hold the position of Chief Information Officer with a small manufacturing company in the southeastern United States.

Here's the basic concept for my part of the story:

- I'm writing this story so my ideas will be the good ones.
- Any descriptions of me or my ideas will not be the comical part of this story.
- I always have everyone's best interest at heart.
- That's my story and I'm sticking with it.

My approach to the job is relatively simple:

1. Identify the problems and/or needs of our clients (our clients are defined as every member of our company & our external clients)
2. Recommend and/or implement solutions
3. Communicate
4. Assess the aftermath

As a CIO I've spent a lot of time educating myself on hardware and software. I've also spent a tremendous amount of time working at assessing needs, developing solutions, defining business processes, building teams, motivating, communicating, implementing, training and evaluating results. One of the most important things I've learned is that without the full support and understanding of the entire management team (especially the top management) nothing can be accomplished. I do understand that a big part of my job is to communicate. That's right, I'm a CIO and I'm talking about communication. ROI, ERP, WTF, BA, BS, BFD, MBA, IP, MAPS RBL, CAD, MCSE, TGIF, MCP, CCNA… is this any way to communicate?

Some communication actually requires the use of real words. Good communication requires that the parties involved actually pay attention to some of the details. Details are something most of us don't really like to deal with. We seem to want the fast food version of everything and we want it at fast food prices. To get anyone to make the investment in the details you've got to first communicate the value. Communication; let's give it a shot.

Today's issue: The joys of being on a "blacklist". If you are ever blacklisted, the joys and rewards you will experience will be similar to those our company has been exposed to. Here is the short list:

1. Emails sent from our company to our clients in Germany were not getting through. They never arrived.
2. In an effort to stop SPAM the emails from our company were being blocked.
3. This practice was being done with no notice to the users.
4. We had to follow set procedures to be removed from the "blacklist".
5. This process would take (at a minimum) from 1 week to 10 days.

Finding the original cause of a problem and following it to a resolution offers me a personal satisfaction and is one the reasons I chose IT as a profession. I enjoy the thrill of the hunt. Unfortunately, I now faced a situation where the hunt was over.

As part of the resolution to our current problem I had to enlist the understanding and support of the Sales department and in particular the head of the Sales department, Larry. Larry and his home computer system were the reason we had ended up on the "blacklist". He's not going to want to hear that at all.

"It's broke. Fix it and fix it now." That phrase would express Larry's and his staff's perspective on this issue. They really believe that the only appropriate response from someone from in IT should be, "I'm fixing it; I'll be done in an hour." I've been told by Larry "I don't want to have to know your job to run this stupid computer. I just want you to help me get my job done." I had to get into the details of the problem and its root cause with people who really didn't want to be bothered.

I was about to enter our company's Sales department meeting. I was going to attempt to communicate, let them know our status, ask for their concerns and questions. Who was I kidding, this is the ultimate "fast food" group in our company and I wasn't bringing fries. They don't want to hear this. They just want their fries.

I thought of the cast of characters that I had seen on the agenda for this meeting and who I was going to be dealing with.

There was:

- Larry Lips, VP of Sales, from a fine New England school, tops in his class, quirky but likeable (especially by our CEO), good golfer, pretty good drinker, doesn't know much about sales and/ or marketing, not enough sense to get out of the rain but he does know a thing or two about self preservation.
- Eddie is one of our engineers. He puts in the hours that make him appear to be a company man and a go getter. Eight PM on a Friday night and you might find him at his desk. If anyone checks to see what he's actually doing they would find he's spending about 69% of his time online sitting on his American Sexual Services.com home page (an adult entertainment site) or playing a computer game. He's doing it at the office because the internet connection is so much faster than his home connection. He thinks that he has everyone convinced of his dedication and that no one has any idea how he spends much of his time at work. He has even made a helpdesk request to have the company pay for a faster internet connection at his home so he won't have to spend so much time at work. He always has a lot of projects under way but I don't think he's ever finished one. He knows that I've looked into his level of expertise and found him to be more of a cup of advice than a wealth of knowledge. He's fully aware that as long as I'm in charge of the

IT department he won't be a part of it. I'm sure he has a BS in something and I'm sure he is dangerous.

I knew this would be fun so I hurried to the Monday morning Sales department meeting. I often hurry to root canals.

I stood up to begin my portion of the Sales meeting stating, "We have found and removed a virus from a computer system attached to our network. The infected system had sent out large amounts (500 to 1000 per day) of SPAM (unsolicited email) to everyone in our company, and to most of our clients. To most of the world these emails would appear to have come from our company. A known virus caused this problem. Our current protection policies and procedures will protect us in the future if we simply use them as directed."

In anticipation of the obvious security concerns and the questions that were about to come I quickly added, "If we had followed those same protection policies and procedures in the past we wouldn't be dealing with these problems." I asked for everyone's support in following those policies and procedures. The lack of any response was further indication that this group wasn't going to "play well with others". Despite the lack of a buy-in I continued, "Due to the amount of SPAM generated by the infected systems we have been placed on a "blacklist" in Germany."

I explained that in efforts to stop Spam organizations such as MAPS RBL (Mail Abuse Prevention System Realtime Blackhole List) had created what are called "blacklist". Anti-spam blacklisting groups, such as MAPS and ORBs, put pressure on ISPs to conform to a set of anti-spam policies and they pressure other ISPs to adopt those same policies. It is estimated that over 50% of US-based ISPs and up to one third of global ISPs already participate in the blacklisting. While blacklists are created with good intentions they sometimes result in a large number of Internet service providers (ISPs) surreptitiously blocking large amounts of non-spam from innocent people. This is because they block all email from entire IP address blocks— companies and even from entire nations. Our entire company was currently being blocked by some ISPs in Germany. This practice is done with no notice to the users.

I voiced that I was in agreement with organizations such as the EFF (Electronic Frontier Foundation) in the belief that the two most popular strategies for combating SPAM (legislation and anti-spam blacklists) have failed. I further expressed that my hopes for the future were that the focus of any efforts to stop SPAM by any organizations should include protecting end users. We need to ensure that all non-SPAM messages reach their intended recipients.

The reality of the situation today was that we were on a "blacklist". We must follow the steps required so that we might be removed from the "blacklist". I assured everyone that our IT department was taking all the appropriate steps to resolve this matter and that it would take a week to 10 days. I offered instructions as to how anyone could send email to our German clients through the use of our helpdesk. I expressed that I had already sent out several emails with that same information and those same assurances to the entire company.

I looked for eye contact with anyone and everyone as I asked if anyone had any questions and/or comments on this or any IT issues. It looked to me like I had already lost everyone's attention. I wanted desperately to let everyone at this meeting know that I understood their current problems and that I and my staff were trying to help them. I wanted to let them know that I shared their pain as our company was losing sales and that IT issues are not what our Sales department needs to deal with. I and my staff wanted to make sure that things like this "blacklist" would never happen again. I never got the chance to express any of those things. Have you ever looked at the expression on a group of sixth grade kids as the teacher wishes them the best over their spring break? This group was already gone. I could only hope we had made some progress. I looked at Larry and said "I've got another meeting so I'll talk with you later. We all count on you folks and I hope you know you can count on your IT department."

Larry said, "Thanks for your help and for coming to let us know what's up." I headed out the door.

The last thing I overheard as I left the Sales meeting was "Don't let those guys in IT tell you that, "blacklist"... what's that? I can go home and send an email from my home computer to our German client right now. We just can't send an email from the system here and that's the responsibility of our IT department. They need to fix it and I mean fix it today!" I recognized that pearl of wisdom came from the voice of Eddie, one of our talented engineers.

Eddie was at the Sales meeting for the purpose of explaining our latest greatest product. This product had been Eddie's project for about nine months now and as was typical of anything he was involved with... it hadn't been finished. He had to address something in his timeslot and I'm sure he thought he had found his scapegoat. Any IT issue is a favorite subject for Eddie as he knows he has just enough IT knowledge to be impressive to most. These limited skills, coupled with his savvy communication skills, prompted Eddie to lodge a complaint about IT at a time then there was no one present to question or respond to his comments. Addressing this issue in this manner removed the focus from Eddie's own ineptness, allowed him to appear to be part of the group in their common complaint and offered Eddie as someone with some level of expertise. Timing is everything.

Eddie is a wiz at heart. It's weird that he feels he should audition for an IT job at the Sales department meeting. I'm sure he's feeling pressure from his long list of unfinished projects and needs new job opportunities. He is a political creature.

No sooner had Eddie finished his statement than Jane jumped to his support, "We ought to let Eddie work on it. He put some new software on my computer last week and its working great. IT had me on a schedule for the install and he just came by and got it done in 5 minutes. He's really good on computers."

Jane, how could I have forgotten about her? I'll introduce her to you now. I generally like what I know of her. I don't know much about her knowledge as we've never had an in depth conversation. I'm not sure she's looking for or is capable of an in depth conversation. I am sure she was somebody's homecoming queen. There's a picture of her with a crown on her head sitting on her desk. She makes it very clear she should be first on everyone's list. I know that when we go to a trade show and she works our booth as our front person, we've always got a line of people around the corner. Don't get me wrong, I'm not judging her but we're talking about her judgment of someone's technical skills. I doubt if she really knows if something was installed correctly or not. I think what she meant to say was "Eddie's really good on computers because he got it done when I asked for it."

I didn't close the door completely, as I expected to hear Larry offer a response or some statement of support for my department. Larry was fully aware of the efforts we were making to address these issues. At the very least I expected Larry to support the company's policies and procedures. It seemed like forever, but as I waited by the door I realized that a statement of support from Larry wasn't coming.

I started to reenter the Sales meeting but Joel, another salesperson, had already started a presentation. I thought it best to address this issue with Larry somewhere other than in front of his entire department. I left the door slightly ajar and headed back to my office. As I walked down the hall I realized that I now had bigger problems than I had imagined. Not only did I have some technical problems. I had "people" problems. These are huge problems to overcome. The "blacklist" issue was small in comparison.

I had gone to this meeting to address one issue and four other issues had emerged. Talk about a fish out of water. I felt like we had been speaking different languages.

I replayed the conversations in my mind.

Didn't I say, "Normally a company is on a blacklist because of not following its own processes and policies?"

Didn't I say, "We can't as business professionals expose our own clients and others businesses to viruses and other dangers?"

Didn't I close with, "We will do whatever is needed to have our company removed from any and all blacklist ASAP but we have to stop causing the problems ourselves?"

Had I not spoken clearly and concisely? Should I have used smaller words, less details, shorter sentences, more pictures, crayons, construction paper?

Yes, I had been speaking the same language and yes, I had addressed what I thought were the issues. I pondered how to better communicate these issues but quickly began to focus again on the current blacklist issue. It was, after all, the first time I had made an attempt to explain face to face to non-technical staff what a blacklist is, how a company gets on a blacklist and how it would affect our company. As for Larry and management, I had to find a time and place to address the issues of mutual support and understanding required to make things work. After all that was my job... to make things work.

My attendance to this Sales meeting was not unusual. I always attended other department staff meetings in an effort to further the support and understanding between departments and throughout our company. At these meetings I would attempt to assess needs, develop solutions, define business processes, build teams, motivate, communicate, and assess results. In this particular meeting I had tried to consider the added pressures that our Sales department might be under, especially with the current business environment. Given the results of this meeting, I couldn't quite remember why I needed to believe in Larry. I didn't hear a lot to believe in at this meeting. I do remember why... I've got to believe in the team I work with.

As I sat at my desk I thought about the current business environment we were facing. The truth of the matter was that during Larry's tenure as VP of Sales our company had gone from 3.5 Million in annual sales to 55 million and back down to 5 million. Sounds like Larry started slow, learned a bit and then had a bout with Alzheimer's doesn't it? Our products were in very high demand and that demand just fell off. I mean it fell off the edge of the earth. No longer were our products selling themselves. Larry now had to rely on his own skills and the skills of his staff.

Larry's staff could best be described as order takers, "Cowboys" or, at the very least, people with the credentials that would cause them to appear to be fine members of our corporate family. Unfortunately they hadn't taken the time to build relationships with our clients. They were too busy counting the money. These folks had ridden a technology boom that had been the driving force behind our years of tremendous growth. It was clear that technology wasn't the real problem for these folks.

Our virus protection strategies (when used) were working. Our business processes and policies were sound and functional (when followed). The blacklisting was, in fact, keeping us from potentially damaging ourselves, our own clients and other systems. Technology was forcing us to address the problem. The difficult issue of trying to communicate the fact that we were our own worst enemy wasn't going so well. Larry didn't want to hear this and neither did his staff. They were too involved with their own issues. In evolution you kill the weak and eat them don't you? Larry's staff was scared. They were ready to eat their young. It was clear to me that we needed to fix our communication problems. You know; all the communications skills you expect from a CIO. It was our job and we had to fix them.

Fix what?

1. I needed to regain the support of all of upper management.
2. I needed upper managements understanding of what IT does and why.
3. Our company had to be able to use our own system to send email correspondence to anyone.
4. We had to get our company off of the blacklist.
5. We needed to follow our own processes and policies.
6. We needed to stop unauthorized installations of software.

As an immediate action, my first task was to communicate to all of our company's staff that my staff and I were aware of the problem and actively working on it. I had already sent one email out to the entire company which gave our status on the "blacklist" issue. I also included, in that same email, instructions as to how we could currently send email to our clients in Germany. As soon as I got back to my office that email was sent out again.

It was time for lunch with my staff and a much needed break. I was looking forward to their input.

I stepped over to my network administrator's office and asked, "Are you guys ready for lunch?"

"In about 20 minutes, we're working on something," replied Carl.

As a network administrator Carl was second to none. Carl is the type of man that takes personal pride in his systems, his work, his clients and his team. If there was a problem and he was aware of it, you didn't have to ask for help… he was on it and stayed on it until it was resolved. He understood his clients were our staff and our company's clients. He took great pride in taking care of them. On the other hand he wasn't shy about sharing his true feelings in our staff meetings.

There was some noise in the hall. It was Carl, Paul (our database administrator) and Henry (our helpdesk technician).

Paul had about 5 years experience prior to coming on board with us. Like Carl if there was a problem and Paul was aware of it, you didn't have to ask, he was on it. He was good, followed instructions well and rarely stuck his neck out.

Henry was fresh out of college and one of those wonderful boot camp graduates. He had great scores on his test for certification, which I believe, caused him to be overconfident at first. That got him into some minor problems during the first six weeks as a member of our team. His response when that happened was impressive as he was good at admitting his mistakes and eager to learn. He was finding the true value that comes from training, hands on experience and working with a crew like ours.

That's the kind of staff we have and I take pride in our department. We headed out of the office to our usual spot where we could have some food and a staff meeting.

After the food and some small talk I began our meeting by asking Carl where we stood on the blacklist problem.

Carl started with a review of his prior actions where he basically confirmed the problems associated with the ("blacklist", communications, policies and procedure) issues we currently faced and how we might address them.

My stomach turned flips as Carl continued "We have spent way too much time and too many of our resources checking to see why our system has been blocking a ton of email (500 to 1000 a day). While that junk appeared to be coming from various sources it was in fact coming from Larry's home office computer. We tracked his IP address. The virus was searching Larry's contact list and randomly choosing who to send from and to. It attaches itself to every email it sends out. This is a known virus and this whole thing could have been avoided if he had just followed our policies and procedures. Larry told Paul that he had noticed his home system had been sending out a lot of email lately, about 1000 a day. He hadn't requested our help or checked with us at all. He said it was his personal home computer. He said his family was using it and Eddie had fixed it so he could work remotely. He's not going to put the blame for this mess on our department. He said he didn't want to bother us. He got Eddie to set this mess up. He and Eddie are bothering me."

I brushed my hair back with my hand and leaned back in my chair. "Larry knows better. As for Eddie, he needs to do his job and quit causing us problems. We have policies and processes already defined for home access and they're not worth a dime if we don't use them."

Paul added, "Eddie's doing this on purpose. He wants our job. They're letting him audition for our job. They want to see just what he can and can't do. Why aren't we enforcing our own policies? We should fire him for violating company policies. That's what it says in the policy. What's the point?"

Henry said, "Those guys are blaming us for this whole "blacklist" mess. This isn't right!"

"You guys know me better. I'm Carl and I'm not going to be held responsible for their stupidity. This is crap and we can't go on like this."

I was in full agreement but as part of the management team I had to respond with, "We have the support where it matters, with Rick. I'm going to set up a meeting with him and we'll get this back on track."

Paul added "I told Larry I needed to see his system again and I went to his house this morning while you were in the Sales meeting. The virus protection was turned off on his system so I turned it back on and checked out the rest of the setup. I just did that same thing last Friday. Someone has been back on his system and they've been playing around. Larry can't be the one be doing it because he doesn't know enough to be doing this type of stuff. He was infected again and was sending out at least 500 to 1000 emails a day to and from everyone in his contact list. He has a remote session set up to his desktop and he is using his name as his user name and our company name as his password. I've told him that user names and passwords need to be harder for someone to guess but he's not changing it."

Carl laughed out loud as he turned to me and said, "That's probably hard enough for Larry to remember as it is. We've got to get these guys and in particular Eddie to stop violating our company policies and processes. It's putting the whole system in danger not to mention it's undermining everything we are trying to do. We can't get our company off of a "blacklist" if we are going to continue to be a danger to ourselves and to others out on the net. The "blacklists" are there to protect people from dangers just like this."

"I understand and I've got to schedule a meeting with Rick. Let me assure each of you that we will get the support we need from the top management in this company. I think we'll all see that we have that support soon. I'll be bringing these issues up at the management meeting tomorrow morning. Meanwhile, are we still on the same timeframe to resolve the current problems and for us to be off the "blacklist"?"

Carl replied, "If we don't have any other Cowboys out there doing whatever they want we can get off the list in about a week to 10 days."

I replied "I just want to make sure we don't have any other surprises. I know Larry and Eddie have to stop.

Henry asked, "Do these guys even see this as a security issue?"

I struggled with my answer, "I'm not sure they are seeing it as anything but a power struggle or an issue that they can use as a scapegoat. They've got a lot of pressure on them and I've got to get them to see the real issues involved."

Paul added, "You do know that Eddie has installed software on Jane's system don't you? He should be fired for that. I mean we have a policy that clearly states no unauthorized installation of software or hardware."

"Jane mentioned it just as I was leaving the Sales meeting. She said it was working great. I understand that we all have legitimate concerns over Eddie and his actions and I'm going to address those issues. It is written in our company policy that these types of actions are a potential reason for termination. As for firing Eddie for those actions that's not my call. You know my position on this. We will just have to wait and see what happens. Thanks for keeping me informed."

Paul replied, "I don't think you know the whole story there. Every time Jane attempts to shut down her machine a screen pops and displays a message that states Eddie is the best. Don't you just love Eddie?"

"You know Paul, Eddie is probably just trying to get a girl, any girl, to remember his name. He is determined to push this issue to the front isn't he? Our company doesn't need to have someone as destructive as Eddie hanging around here. Thanks for the info. I will deal with Eddie. It sounds like you guys are doing what I and the company need. You have some legitimate concerns. I have a list of things we all need to look at. I think you'll see we are all on the same page." It was apparent that my staff was feeling pressure and lack of support. I felt proud that they were still working towards resolutions and working as a team.

Here's the list I handed to my staff:

- Craig needs to regain the understanding & support of all of upper management.
- We had to get our company off of blacklist.
- We must be able to use our own systems to send email and conduct normal business correspondence to anyone.
- We needed to have everyone in our company follow our own processes and policies.
- We needed to stop unauthorized installations of software and hardware.

I watched everyone's facial expressions while they read the list and felt good as I could tell that we were all on the same page. I was keenly aware that some destructive actions had already occurred within our company and that they were very serious. We were sitting on a bomb. The good news was that I was working with an IT staff that knows what to do to fix things and still cares enough to want to do it. They had shown me that they want to do whatever it takes to get things done. Now it was my job to get the other members of our company on board. We discussed some other matters and then we all headed back to work.

As I sat down at my desk, I realized… it was still Monday. This day just kept dragging on. What I had thought to be a manageable problem (the blacklist problem) had only been a symptom that now exposed the much greater problems. If I couldn't communicate and receive the support and understanding from our company's management, I had no hope of addressing any issues of security or anything else. My job in this particular instance had little to do with technical matters but everything to do with communications and commitment. My experiences from the past gave me reason for concern as I have seen technology become an easy scapegoat to cover real issues like, dropping sales, poor business plans, processes etc.

I did find some solace as I remembered the comments our CEO had made when he hired me as he had stated, "Craig, I'm bringing you into our family to enlist your help so that we might (for the first time in our company) have a structured, accountable system. We all understand that if we don't do these things we will not succeed. You have my personal support one hundred percent (100%)."

With that positive thought still fresh in my mind I called Larry's extension to see if we could chat together about some of these issues before we had the Tuesday management meetings.

Larry was quick to respond "30 minutes".

It was exactly 30 minutes later as I was standing outside Larry's office, when I overheard Jerry (our lead salesman who sees himself as the driving force of our company) and Larry talking.

Jerry stated, "Eddie has sent some emails for me as I still can't get an email sent from our system. Eddie's getting more IT stuff done for me than our entire IT staff. What are we paying those guys for? I've probably lost sales because they've messed up our email. You can't hold me accountable for lost sales because we look like idiots when we can't even send an email from our own system."

"Jerry you know that I can't send anything to Germany either don't you? If Eddie can get your email out let me know. Maybe he can get these messages out for me today. I don't know what's going on with our system. Tell Eddie to come see me ASAP."

About that time Larry caught sight of me standing outside his door and he said, "Craig is here. Maybe he's got some good news for us. Jerry's done so come on in Craig."

As he walked out Jerry's comment was "Are you gonna help me get my job done?"

I quickly responded, "I have always tried to help you."

As Jerry walked away I pulled the door to Larry's office closed and sat down. "Larry I need your help so I can better serve you and your staff."

"Craig, your systems aren't working and they're causing us to lose sales. You need to understand that we can't afford to lose one sale. It's that simple. I heard you talking about how we caused ourselves to get on this blacklist thing and frankly I don't really understand. What I do understand is I can't sit at my desk and send an email to my German client. I can't see that you're serving me at all right now."

"First of all, Larry, you can send an email out to our clients in Germany. You can use the computer that is sitting on your desk and you can do it right now. There hasn't been a moment in time that you couldn't do that. Didn't you read the email I sent out? It tells everyone how to send emails to Germany until we get this problem taken care of. Didn't Paul find out that your new home computer was infected with a virus that's sending out tons of infected emails? Paul also explained to you that to anyone outside of our company those emails appear to be coming from us?"

"Paul did say something about my system but I'm not sure what he was talking about. It doesn't matter anyway because your guys didn't work on that system. Eddie set that up for me. He's really good at computers. You really ought to look at bringing him into your department."

My dilemma at this point was Larry's perception of the problem. I tried a new approach, "Larry, what would you do if you a guy in the computer department called up one of our clients and started giving prices out on our products? This person then posts a list of those prices on our web site for anyone to see and tells all of the other salespersons that I had authorized him to do these things."

As he leaned back in his chair Larry snapped, "That's ridiculous... what's your point?"

I continued with my analogy. "Let's take it further, Larry. You discover that all of this has occurred and you come to me for support. I respond to you by saying I think I've got a new pricing scheme that one of my IT folks figured out. I think you ought to give it a look. You ought to look at adding him to your sales staff."

"Did you come in here to have a pissing contest? What's your point, Craig? We all need these systems to do our job and it's your job to keep them going."

Larry had just gotten the point... or at least he'd said it out loud even if he didn't understand it. For the first time, I felt that there was a chance to get through to him. I stated, "That's exactly my point Larry. It's your job to get the sales department going and mine to keep the technology running. We have those jobs because we each have expertise in those areas."

I quickly continued, "It is critical that you and I communicate, understand and respect each other's roles and responsibilities. We both have to know and believe in each other. We have to work together. If we are counting on a "Wiz" like Eddie to run our business we might as well flush, because we are done. Let's clear up what we need to, define what we both bring to the table and get this business running again. When it comes to our security, technology, business processes and policies I need your support and the support of everyone here. Let me give you a list to summarize what we all have to do to solve these issues."

I handed Larry this list:

1. We must stop all practices of sending emails with non-supported machines.
2. All of our staff must use operating systems supported by our IT department.
3. Everyone must use current anti-virus protection at all times.
4. We all must follow our own business processes and policies.
5. Stop all unauthorized installations of software and/or hardware.
6. Any use of any company IT systems (as defined in our policies) will be subject to all of the terms and conditions contained in our written policies. That does include the disciplinary actions as stated in our written policies and procedures.

"When we accomplish all of the above we will get our company off of the "blacklist". If we work together we will stay off of these "blacklist". These things exist on the internet to protect other internet users from irresponsible companies that would endanger themselves and others by not following simple and prudent policies of normal business operations. We can do this together."

Larry leaned back in his chair and rolled a golf ball in his hand. I could tell he'd had about all of the information he could handle for today. "Craig, my folks are just frustrated, they don't understand and I'm not sure I really do. If I can give them a date as to when we can clean up this mess I'll try to get their buy in. We'll go from there."

Feeling it was the best I was going to get, I stated with a smile, "Great, you can count on my support. I am telling my folks that we have the best group of sales professionals we could find working on our sales issues. I hope that you're reassuring your staff that the best IT staff you've ever seen is working hard to help solve technical issues. As for a date when we will get off of the "blacklist", it's the same as in the email, a week to 10 days. That is if you'll let us handle your home computer and no one else causes us problems. You know, we might find some outside activity like golf or bowling where our staffs might bond a bit. We could build some teamwork if we do something like that at least once every other month or so."

Larry's surprise was evident but he did reply, "Sounds good, I'll get back to you on that."

I headed towards the door. "Thanks for your help, Larry. I'll get on with the process of getting us off of the blacklist. Please send helpdesk request for anything you or your folks need. I'll keep an eye on how the responses go. Thanks again. If you see Eddie let him know that I'd like to see him ASAP."

As I was walking back to my office I came upon Eddie in the hall. "Eddie, I need your help in making sure that only authorized persons install hardware and software on our systems."

His response was short, "You guys weren't getting to it so I tried to help. What's wrong with that? IT doesn't have to control everything."

Eddie's response was further evidence that he had an agenda that was all his own. He didn't understand or care what our problems were. He didn't care what we were trying to do to solve them. He obviously felt he had the freedom and the support to go against company policy and procedures. We parted knowing that this conversation wasn't over.

As I sat down at my desk I dialed Rick's extension.

Connie (Rick's secretary) answered, "Hello how may I help you?"

"Connie this is Craig. I really need a favor. Could you get me a few moments of Rick's time this afternoon before he leaves?"

"You're in luck. I can get you in for 30 minutes if you can come right now."

Standing up as I spoke I said, "Connie you're a doll and I'm on my way."

As I neared his office Rick came rushing out of his door and said, "Go on in and have a seat I'll be right back."

As I sat down in his office I did have a brief moment where the thought "Do I have his support?" crossed my mind. Before I had any more time for that Rick returned and closed the door.

As he sat in his chair I could see the concern on his face. "Ohhhh Craig... We do have a problem don't we?"

"Yes we..."

Rick interrupted, "I'm getting a lot of complaints about our email system. I gotta tell ya, Craig, it makes us look very unprofessional when we can't even send an email to our clients. How did you let this happen? We've spent a ton of money on security and stuff you recommended to avoid this kind of mess."

I thought to myself this is same guy who'd said, "Craig, I'm bringing you into our family to enlist your help so that we might (for the first time) have a structured, accountable system." I also thought of my comment to my staff earlier in the day when I said, "We have the support we need, Rick". I was about to find out if any of those thoughts were based in reality.

"Did you get a chance to read any of the emails I have sent out to everyone concerning the "blacklist" problem?" As Rick leaned towards me with I noticed a small bead of sweat on his forehead. I've never seen him sweat. Come to think of I'd never seen him yell, curse, or laugh. I realized that this wasn't going well. I'd relied on the words of support from someone I didn't even know.

Rick said "I didn't see the email but Larry mentioned something to me about a "Blacklist". Craig, we're not talking about joining the country club here, we're talking about sending a simple email. It's one of the ways we do business. I hired you to build us a secure system that would let us do our job. It doesn't appear that we have one. You and your staff need to get this fixed and fixed now. I mean before we had our own internal mail servers and this elaborate system we could always send emails through the local internet provider… do we need to go back to that?"

This meeting was not going well. That was an understatement. I had to communicate with him. I really had nothing to lose. "OK, I'll be happy to be held responsible for my actions or for those of my department. I will not be held responsible for what others are or are not doing. I didn't let this problem occur but I am attempting to fix it. If you'll give me the authority I'll make sure this is fixed and doesn't ever happen again."

I took a breath and continued, "First of all I need to fire Eddie. He has violated our company policies. He has been playing computer games and browsing adult web sites on company time, running around installing software and hardware, all of which are against our company policies. He installed a system at Larry's home and forgot to make sure the anti virus software was on it. Larry, you know our VP of Sales, I have to fire him too. He had Eddie work on his system instead of asking our IT staff to set it up to attach to our network here. Those actions have caused us to be on the "blacklist". We're on that list because Larry's home machine was sending out 500 to 1000 junk emails a day that all looked to the rest of the world like they were coming from our network. I can solve the IT problems we're having but the real solution to these issues involves dealing with these two individuals. By firing these guys, or at least taking some disciplinary action, we will set an example to the rest of our staff that we have policies and procedures for a reason. We have to show that there are some consequences when they are violated. Have you even read our policies?"

I didn't wait for an answer as I added, "While we are at it, in the management meeting tomorrow I will once again and for the last time instruct everyone that any IT issues not put through the helpdesk will not be resolved. As a matter of fact they won't even be discussed. I'll leave it up to you if you would like to add that the helpdesk is the only method we have to measure the effectiveness, needs and the results of our IT department."

As I continued my ranting I fumbled for my current helpdesk report, which I found and threw on the desk, "The IT department, which is very probably your best department in this company, is measured in this documented report. We have responded and resolved 83% of all helpdesk requests within 4 hours and another 5% within 8 hours. The remaining (12%) of all other helpdesk request range from two days to two weeks with the exception of longer term projects. Any and all helpdesk request also receive an automated response, which is for the verification of the person making the request that their request has been received. Anyone in this company can use the helpdesk system to prove whether or not the IT department is responding. Without these kinds of systems, policies and procedures, we cannot and I will not function. Without this kind of structure and accountability we are dealing with perceptions not reality. How do you measure a perception? We are not talking about technology but the simple fact we that we have self-inflicted wounds. You're the CEO... are you just gonna stand around and watch us bleed to death? If you won't do what's needed give me the authority. I'm not here to be your cop but I will help you build a team second to none."

As Rick held the helpdesk report, he looked a bit overloaded with info. "So you're telling me 88% of the time your folks are getting the request done to the point where the user that requested the action states a positive result." As he spoke those words I saw something I had never seen in Rick before. It was fear.

"That's exactly what I'm saying, Rick. There are some exceptions. Unfortunately some of our folks have just decided not to use helpdesk. As for those staff members that have chosen not to use helpdesk, I don't want to hear their comments. If anyone really believes that their helpdesk request isn't being responded to, they need to use helpdesk itself to prove it. Show up with a request, an automated verification and evidence of no response; or I don't want to hear it. We need to make good use of our Helpdesk, our policies and procedures. We need to constantly assess the results, communicate and improve. Rick, I came to you today to get the support you told me I would have when you hired me. I've done a quality job to this point. I need and deserve your support. The whole company and I need you to take a stand on these issues. I would hope that could start right now and that you would voice it at our management meeting tomorrow."

Rick was looking very tired. "I'm sorry, Craig, I didn't mean to go off on you but things need to get back on track around here. We've got a sales department looking in any direction for a scapegoat. They're making destructive comments about other departments like design, accounting and yes your folks in IT too. They're not alone as some folks are looking at those folks in sales as our problem. We've got to pull this ship together and start rowing together and we need to do it now. I'll trust in you that we're on track with the IT issues. I will try to read your email on the "blacklist" but can you just tell me where we are on sending emails out of here?"

"We have always been able to send email to Germany if we follow the instructions in the email I sent out. You're upset over perceptions and not seeing the reality of the situation. We need your leadership and support. It looks like we can get back to normal methods of sending email in a week to 10 days but the bottom line is no one has ever been prevented from sending email to Germany or anywhere. They just need to send it to helpdesk with the intended destination and we will get it forwarded. That's the best we can do until we get removed from the "blacklist". Getting off of a "blacklist" is not something I can control other than to follow the procedures that are required."

Rick's response was almost as vague as his expression, "That's all I really needed. I will read your email. Is there anything else, Craig?"

Seeing the pressure he was under in a new light, I questioned his leadership as never before. "No, there's nothing else right now. Let me know if you have any questions after you read the email. Thanks for your time." As I headed for my office I desperately tried not to think about what had just occurred, as it would only cause me to further my search for leadership in a person that, for right now at least, I still needed to believe in.

As I sat down at my desk I clicked on the icon that produces my weekly report to show me our network activity. It allows me to allocate resources where needed and in general help our heavy users and avoid problems. I noticed our heaviest user for the third week in a row was Uranus Thumb our Sales representative for Croatia. I checked to see what type of activities he was in that would cause him to be using that kind of bandwidth. To my surprise the women from Croatia are quite attractive, friendly and a bit kinky... or so it appears. It's Monday, my name is Craig, I'm the CIO here and I'm going home now.

ID10T Errors

---

1. The "Blacklist", SPAM problem.

According to some estimates as much as 60% of the email traffic on the internet is SPAM (unsolicited bulk email). You didn't ask for it but you're getting e-mails about increasing the size of your penis or your breast, buying prescription drugs online or making $1,000.00 a week from home. The motives for spammers to send millions of e-mails are simple: money. The security risks and costs associated with these types of activities are increasing. There are all kinds of SPAM blockers available and unfortunately none really work (100%) for every situation.

"Blacklists" are a good example of how we occasionally make mistakes with well-intended efforts to control or correct bad things. Some Blacklist sites such as ORBZ (Open Relay Blocking Zone), have even been shut down because of criminal charges for denial of service. In our story, the "blacklist" was trying to protect others from a virus we were sending out. The "blacklist" was also denying our company the right to communicate with our clients in Germany. Until the time comes when we find better solutions, we need to be aware of the user and the situation. We have to rely on the tools available, our own expertise or the experts we choose.

2. Improper use of user names and passwords.

Although a small security problem in this story, Larry's dangerous use of his name and his company's name as user name and password poses serious security risks. There are many schemes you could use to be more secure. The point here being that the more difficult it is for someone to guess you user name and password, the more secure your system. Another aspect of this type of security concern would be the amount of time and/or attempts you would allow someone to have in gaining access to your network.

More secure schemes might:

1. Require a user name to include a combination of numeric and alpha characters.
2. Require passwords to change every 30 to 90 days.
3. Lockout user after three invalid login attempts.
4. Limit the amount of time someone has to attempt access.

3. Every company has to actually have a leader.

The number one security issue in this story was a lack of leadership. Without strong leadership you will have no security at all. A company cannot have policies, procedures or effective systems without leadership. Policies, procedures, systems and security issues should be a reflection of the leadership in a company. Once established there should also be methods by which all of these tools would have their results measured. Those measurements should be used to affect change and reward successes. The company in our story had written policies and procedures but did not enforce them. They were useless. They had systems, but not the structure to use them properly. A company that would allow people to do the things the characters in this story did would very likely become a victim of SPAM, vandalism, credit card fraud, identity theft or corporate espionage. Where's the structure? Where's the accountability? The company in our story was out of control.

Craig made some serious errors. He counted on support and understanding that wasn't there. He sought it at a critical time and it wasn't to be found. Craig's comment that he didn't know Rick, the person that was most important to his support and understanding, told a lot about his own chances for survival and his own lack of communication skills. Prior to the events in this story Craig should have invested in the relationship with Rick so that the two of them would have had a stronger relationship from which to draw. Craig seemed to think that doing a good job and doing it for the right reasons should be enough to get the type of support and understanding he needed. Big mistake.

4. Every company needs an SOB.
    (Or at the very least you should rent one from time to time.)

Someone has to be in charge. Enforcement of your own policies and procedures gives them value. I'm not talking about extremes. I simply believe that most people want to work together and will do well if:

   a. You let them know where the boundaries are.
   b. Where you need help.
   c. What the rewards are for compliance.
   d. What the consequences are for violation.
   e. You are consistent.

5. Communication.

The serious lack of communications, that was so painfully evident in our story, was the second biggest problem our company had. The lack of good communications threatens not only security issues but the very existence of this company. Relationships are born of communication. Relationships are normally built during good times and tested during bad times. The ones that start during bad times usually involve a change in the parties involved. From the lack of relationships we see in this story it's probably best that somebody's going to have a career change. If it continues as a house of cards it will surely crumble from its own weight.

Craig, Larry and Rick had not taken the time to nurture their relationships. Those relationships weren't strong enough to offer the respect, trust and support needed to make it through the hard times the company was facing.

If the interactions between Craig and Eddie don't improve quickly, Eddie will probably find it easy to advance his career. He may, in fact, have found an environment where his bluffs work. We've all seen companies where perceptions are the reality. Eddie was taking full advantage of that situation in our story. He was putting in the hours and it looks as if he will succeed. If the perception is you're a dedicated hard worker, maybe you might be able to just sit on your American Sexual Services.com home page and never have to finish a thing. If that turns out to be the case, Craig may find he has no support from above and none from below. Not a good place to be. His sole harbor of support would then be coming from his department. That is where he has invested his time. Good luck.

As soon as you join a company you need to develop relationships with the people who will provide you with your continuing education, guidance, support and understanding. These people will affect what you do and you will affect them in turn. By investing in these relationships you will be building a team. The investment you make in building that team will pay dividends over and over again to you and every member of that team. In our story Craig had not done that with Rick the CEO or Larry the VP of Sales. When it came time for their support he didn't have it. Even though it appears that Rick is going to support Craig through this "blacklist" issue, the relationship between Craig and Rick and Craig and Larry are damaged. The perception left with Larry and Rick is that when times were tough Craig was part of the problem and added pressure rather than relieved it. Craig may solve the "blacklist" problem, but not the real issue of communication, support and understanding. Those issues not only threaten our company but Craig's own personal security; his job.

Tuesday

I knew I'd be telling my story one day. I had a vision. I'm going to tell you my story with the sincere hope that I can get some therapeutic value from telling it. Things have been a bit stressful lately and I've got to get centered. I normally handle stress very well. This latest bout with stress is different though as it seems to be interfering with my visions. Everything seems to be in chaos and unrest. I'll lie down on the couch now as I begin by telling you about our company and myself. I have always had the gift of being able to see the bigger picture and envision opportunities in the future. That's a big part of the reason that I'm the CEO. Sometimes when I'm talking with staff members I get visions of little messages tattooed across their foreheads. Those messages help me understand what I need to do. You'll see what I mean later. I'm an engineer and this is my company. I know how to motivate people and get things done as is evidenced by our track record. I'm accustomed to success.

Our company was conceived at a meeting between our two parent companies about six years ago. At that meeting there was a lot of discussion about the new product that one of our parent companies had just developed. The demand for this product was incredible but there was a problem with a possible conflict of interest and a potential problem with the ability to market the product in the U.S. since most of the actual manufacturing was being done in China. This became our main product and we have become the sole distributor of this product in the U.S. market.

We started off with a product in extremely high demand (one of our parents gave us an initial order that would keep us busy for the first five years). We were given plenty of capital and I got to pick my own staff members. I went into this company with the highest of expectations. The only people I really have to answer to around here are the members of the "Board" and that's only twice a year.

In my 27 years of business experience I have relied on a sound business philosophy of positive management. I believe and use a positive reinforcement style of management to create a positive environment. I choose not to use negative motivational tools and do not believe in or use confrontation as a motivational tool. I use terms like "Did you get their buy-in?" a lot and I believe this system works. Just look at our track record of non-stop growth ever since our inception. Well, almost non-stop growth. I believe our current downturn is only a bump in the road and not a real reflection of our true business conditions. I've been around long enough to see these types of things through. I know how to get my team's buy-in and how to get us back on track. I believe in surrounding myself with talented people with great expertise, giving them the tools to use their expertise and staying out of their way so that they might get the job done. I do not micro manage. I don't want to be that involved. I expect my people to do what I hired them to do, their job.

As a visionary I really shouldn't have to deal with petty details. I've been to the mountain and I've seen the other side. I've given all of these talented folks whatever they need to get up there on their own. Why are they still bothering me? I've given you way too much insight into my own persona so on with the day's events.

I casually walked down the hall towards our main meeting room. The room itself was a testimony to what I'd given to the members of this company. We had hired the best office designers we could find to give our room the feelings of comfort, creativity and success. The ceiling was sculptured three layers deep for the best aesthetic and acoustic results, the chairs were so comfortable you could sit in them for 3 hours and still have feeling in your butt, the table had built in phones and computer screens, the white board could send information directly to the printers or email, the lights had more available settings than the local community theatre. As I walked into the room I was comforted with the sounds of waves crashing on the beach that came from our sophisticated sound system. How could anyone not be motivated in this room? It's Tuesday morning; time to use this room for our weekly management meeting. As I called the meeting to order my thoughts were scattered, as I hadn't been able to find the answers to the current issues of our dropping sales figures, high cost of carrying inventory items, staff attacking each other and technology issues that no one understood. I tried to convince myself that I had chosen good staff and reassure myself that they would have some answers. I was worried.

My thoughts were interrupted as Craig, our structure based, logic driven, 45 year old CIO said, "Rick, if I could have the floor I'd like to address the email or "blacklist" issue." You could tell from the bulges in his neck that Craig was about to stress out over this.

David, our mild mannered, 34 year old VP of Manufacturing added, "I sure hope you're fixing this mess. Larry told me last week it was costing us sales."

Our bottom line, 38 year old, wizard of numbers, VP of Finance, Jim, added, "We can't lose any sales right now... not one."

Craig responded in a predictable manner. "Slow down folks. If everyone has read their emails than you all know we haven't been prevented from sending emails at all. We do have to send them through helpdesk due to the "blacklist" issues. Let me make it very clear to everyone that we have never been without the ability to send emails to Germany. We have always been able to communicate with our clients."

Joe, 39 years old, a frustrated ex Navy Seal and our Director of Engineering, said, "Craig, I just got off the phone with our folks in Germany and they haven't made the changes that I had asked for. Those changes were in the drawings I sent to them in an email last week. The folks in Denver got the email but the folks in Germany say they never got it."

"Did you send it through helpdesk, Joe? If you didn't send it through helpdesk it probably didn't work. These issues have all been covered in 3 or 4 separate emails, which my staff and I have sent to everyone in the company. We can go over this again in this meeting but we need to communicate better. How big a sign do we need here? Use your helpdesk. Read your email. How about a small wallet sized reminder, construction paper, billboard or a TV ad? Just tell me what will work and I'll do it."

"It's real simple, Craig. We need this fixed. Computers are just a tool we use. They're not working. What are you doing to fix the problem?"

"I'm trying to identify the problems and the reasons why we're having those problems. I'm doing that with the hope that we might learn from our mistakes and avoid these problems next time. Eddie's a big part of the reason we have problems with our email. He's one of your staff members isn't he Joe? He's gone against our policies and caused this mess. Have you done anything to stop this? Do you know what our policies and procedures are? Is that how you build a team?" From the tone of voice and the content of this response I was sure that Craig hadn't remembered that Joe was an ex Navy Seal. I guess he couldn't see that tattoo "born to kill" on Joe's arm.

"Are you kidding me? I have to give Eddie my email messages so he can go through his home system to send them to Germany. He's helping us out. Why are you jumping on him? Why don't you stay in your department and fix your own mess?"

My staff is acting like a pack of spoiled brats. Not one person in this room, this glorious room I'd given them, seemed to be thinking about what they had been given to work with, positive management, teamwork and our company or finding solutions. They were too selfish and too busy attacking each other. I need a time out.

My thoughts wandered away from these infantile battles and back through our company's history. Our company was a joint venture between 2 fortune 500 companies. We were given products to sell, plenty of capital funds for startup, as well as additional funds and staff for growth in the early years. The products we offered even sold themselves (75% of our sales were to one of our parent companies). Three years ago we were experiencing a triple digit growth rate. At that point I used my positive management philosophy and gave everyone new titles, raises, benefits and just about anything they asked for. We all played golf, ate at the best restaurants, had the best equipment, had as many staff members as we wanted and we all traveled first class. We were even working from our own capital resources. Everyone was happy and my positive management style was a success.

When our sales started trending lower we all thought it would turn back around quickly. It hasn't and we're still waiting. Unfortunately, waiting seems to be all we have done as we have burned through most of our resources. We have to find some solutions soon, or I'm the one who will be the child asking the parents for help. I don't want have to go to our Board and ask for capital. I'm the one who is going to look like an idiot in front of the board as I try to explain how we've gotten ourselves into this mess.

I put this team together. I choose to work with these people. They have the right credentials, the experience and supposedly the track records to get this done. Why can't they just work together and do their jobs? The dull roar of these idiots and their verbal free for all continued in the background as I thought, I should have bought tickets, some popcorn and candy as this is quite a show. There are times when I feel I'm the only adult in the room.

Much as I really didn't want to, I had to say something and I had to say it now. "Listen up folks, Craig has already gone over this matter with me and I feel that he and his staff are doing what they can to get this email thing back on track."

Joe interrupted, "Come on Rick, he's attacking one of my best staff members, I have to respond to that. The only thing Eddie has done is try to help. We need more people like Eddie around here."

While Joe was speaking, Craig was busy handing out copies of the company's policies to everyone in the room. Craig's response to Joe was confrontational and didn't offer much hope in our efforts to resolve anything. "Eddie has caused us problems and has gone directly against our own policy. It's right in front of you. Have you read it before?"

"That's enough."

With "Please stop me, I can't stop myself" stamped across his forehead, Craig was relentless. "No it's not Rick. Do we have company policies or not? If we had followed the policies you have right in front of you, we wouldn't have had any of these email issues. We've done this to ourselves. This isn't about technology; it's about policies, procedures and how we all work together. Do we work together?"

I said, "That's enough. Craig you told me this email thing would be solved within a week to 10 days, is that right?"

"Yes we can do that, but only if we can follow our own policies and procedures and nobody else gives us any problems."

There he goes again. Craig always gets stuck on an issue and then buries the entire conversation in the details. He loves details. Most of us really don't care about the details of how an email is sent. We just want it to work! We want to hear Craig say that he will get it fixed and then we want to forget about it. He doesn't get that. He hardly ever uses a positive approach. He needs to learn how to communicate. I've tried to help him but he's getting on my nerves. He needs to offer me solutions not more confrontation and problems. If he ever got his head out of his department and got a view of the big picture he would be a much better CIO. I've got to get him to understand that we have to move on. "Does anyone is this room not understand that we need our email system working and that we need to support whatever Craig says we need to do to get this fixed?"

There was no response. Every person in the room was looking down at paperwork, at their notebook, out the window, at their shoes or anywhere that would take them away from Craig's endless barrage. With his relentless confrontational approach Craig had succeeded in burying the subject and himself in the details. Not one person in this room wanted to hear anything else about the email system. I'm sure it was evident that I was in no mood to get into any further details. If I could just keep these folks on track with the real issues maybe we could turn this company around. The real issues to me are very simple, we need to be able to send emails to Germany, get the sales figures back up, work well together and do our jobs.

I noticed that Larry had been as quiet as a mouse. That's not a good thing as Larry's is a mouth breather. By that I mean his mouth is always open. The only time I've ever seen Larry's mouth shut is when he's done something wrong or is about to do something wrong. It was time to end his silence. "How are our sales figures, Larry? Are we going to meet forecast?".

Larry replied, "Everything is slow, Rick. You just can't get blood out of a stone. We're probably about 30% short for this month. I think we can meet next month's forecast. We need to take a look at the process of how our system is creating the forecast."

As I spoke I heard the frustration slip out in my tone of voice, "Sales, Larry. We need sales. What are you doing about sales?"

Jim added, "At our current rate of sales we are sitting on about three years' worth of inventory. We need to write off some the cost of that inventory and we need to have a sale. That might help us generate some more sales."

"Don't get carried away, Jim. We've never had to discount our products. I think this is all going to turn around within about six months."

"Do you know the cost of carrying that inventory for another six months? If we lower the value of the inventory we can get a tax break and lower our price to our client. We might even sell some."

With "I don't know" written across his forehead, Larry stated firmly, "What are you talking about? We've already paid for that stuff. It's just sitting here until the market recovers. You're new to this market and I can tell you it will come back soon and will come back stronger than ever."

I was forced to put an end to yet another argument, "Let's take this offline. The three of us need to get together this afternoon. I'll let you know when."

Craig stated, "Has everyone had a chance to look at the policies?"

"We're not here to go over our policies, Craig. I don't want to discuss policies. What I do want to hear is you to telling me that you've got the solutions to this email issue. You just need to get our email system working."

"I can't do that without everybody's help. We can't continue to blatantly go against our own policies. We're not solving anything, Rick. I don't want to take this issue offline. I don't want to deal with it later. You're not helping me, you're just stalling. We have everyone we need in this room right now to deal with this issue right here, right now. I want to get us off of the "Blacklist" so our email will work the way you and I want it to. I'm trying to get this resolved and to get us to stop causing our own problems. I need your help, Rick!"

This guy has no perception of just how big of a hole he is digging with me. He probably hasn't even noticed the sarcasm in my voice. "Fine, tell us all just what you need."

As Craig rambled on in what seemed like some sort of mental quicksand of details and computer language my thoughts quickly wandered. I thought to myself, I've got dropping sales figures, a VP of Sales who doesn't understand anything other than his golf score, a financial guy telling me to dump inventory, engineers doing who knows what with my money and their time, a Computer guy demanding we change things and basically an every man and woman for themselves mentality spreading across my sinking ship. I see chaos and destruction. The visions I have for our company are getting blurrier.

My thoughts were interrupted again when Craig asked; "I need everyone's help to keep us from having these types of problems. Rick, do I have your support?"

Even though I hadn't listened to the details I knew that Craig needed me to offer him some sort of support. "I think we all understand what you need and you will get the support you need. We need these emails and our system to work."

I could tell from the glazed looks around the room that whatever Craig had just gone over he certainly hadn't gotten the buy-in of the other members of our management team. What a time for communications breakdown, or a power struggle, or whatever was going on. I wonder if I can take myself offline? When in doubt just keep moving.

It is true it's hard to hit a moving target so I moved as fast as I could on to the next topic, "Joe, has Eddie finished his work on the X-13 Product?"

"No, he's got about 2 more months of work before it will be ready. We had some problems with some suppliers."

"Joe, you know how much we need that product on the market now. We've spent a ton on this and don't have a dime on the return side of the investment."

Craig added, "Maybe you should put somebody on it other than Eddie."

"Keep your damn hands on your computers and stay out of my department. You don't know anything about the skills needed or what it takes to get things done in Engineering. You come to this meeting and try to use my staff as an excuse as to why you can't even keep our systems working. We're supposed to be using a positive style of motivation, Craig. I haven't heard anything but attacks and excuses from you and I'm tired of it."

"I'm just trying to get something solved. I'm not attacking anyone or any department, Joe. I'm not picking on Eddie when I say he has caused us problems. I'm just stating the facts. As for our systems, they are working just fine and I can back that up with helpdesk reports."

To put an end to the destruction, I jumped in again, "I won't tolerate the language or the attitude. Our time is up for today. Here are the action items for everyone. Joe, we need to get together Friday morning to see just what's going on with the suppliers. Larry, Jim and I will meet later today on Sales and Inventory issues. Craig, I want you to send out an email to everyone in the company praising your team for their efforts in finding and working on a solution to our current email problem. I'll finish this meeting on a positive note; let's all pull together and make things better, we've done it before."

On that positive note I ended what was possibly one of the worst meetings I've ever been a part of. No visions here, just a nightmare. I can only hope that I had been convincing and that no one could sense my real feelings. I and everyone else here blamed Craig and his staff for the IT problems. I was just trying to keep them motivated so they would fix the problem. I don't think for a minute that Larry can or will do anything about our sales issues. I do understand that the concept of teamwork is being trashed. I'm not clear on any solutions other than we need more sales at this point. We don't seem to be headed in the right direction. I need to get out of here and regroup.

I noticed that my pace was a bit quicker as I started to leave the room. It wasn't the casual pace I had when this meeting started. As I got close to the door Craig ran up to me and said, "My staff is asking me what is going to happen to Eddie for violating our policies and procedures. What do I tell them?"

"Tell them not to worry about Eddie but to focus on getting the emails flowing in and out of our system. Eddie's not in your department so he's not your staff's concern. You need to show your positive management skills, Craig. We're trying to build a team here. I'm sure Joe will handle Eddie. I've got to go now." Maybe I should have just kicked him.

My pace quickened even more as I walked out the door. Just then I caught a glimpse of Joe, who was smiling at Craig. It wasn't a friendly smile but one of those smiles you used to give your big brother just after you said, "go ahead and tell Dad, I won't get into trouble anyway." If Joe had just stuck his tongue out we would have had a true Norman Rockwell moment. Just let me get to my office and close the door.

As I turned to leave I almost ran into David. "Panic" was written all over his face. "I need you to stop by my office right now if you can."

"I'm really tied up, can't we talk later?"

"This is very important."

I said, "OK, I'll be right there."

It was about 5 minutes later when I opened the door to David's office. He looked up from his desk as I sat down and said, "Thanks for coming. I wouldn't have acted so urgently if this wasn't important."

I said, "No problem, David. What's up? You looked stressed."

"Panic" was still written across his face and his voice shook as he stated, "Are we going bankrupt?"

I laughed, "What?"

"The auditors we've got working on our books right now have been talking loud enough that some of my staff have overheard some scary comments. My folks are worried about the future of our business."

I wasn't happy with what I just heard and it showed in the tone of my voice. "What comments?"

"What they've heard is that we are making huge adjustments to our books just to please the "Board" and that they (the auditors) can't sign off on these types of accounting practices. We're talking about 300K to 500K monthly adjustments. Those are big adjustments for a company that's looking at 5 million in annual sales this year. Are we doing this kind of stuff?"

I said firmly, "Let me start by saying, our company is sound. We have a great product, high demand, a good company and the full strength and support of the "Board". If we should ever need resources other than our own, our parent companies have very deep pockets. You can trust me when I say we are going to be here for a long time."

As I searched his face for the signs of a buy-in I continued with, "As for the current set of auditors that are going over our books right now, these are two new guys that normally work with companies that offer stock to the public. I mention that because we are a privately held company and the accounting rules are different. We aren't subject to SEC type scrutiny when it comes to our books. What we have done and are currently doing is what we need to do. Basically, we just have to please the "Board" with the perception that we are on the right track."

"Panic" was still written all over his face. "I understand about the difference in accounting rules but the mere size of these adjustments scares me. It also scares me that we are paying auditors that don't have a good working knowledge of what they should be doing for us and who they should be talking to. Are those really the size of the adjustments we make to our books on a monthly basis?"

"We have a lot of resources here, David. Most of our capital is tied up in inventory items and equipment. Any adjustments we've made were legal and were made to help us get back to where we need to be. As for the auditors, I'll talk to them. What I need from you is the leadership to assure your staff that we are a sound company and we are going to be here for a long time. They've got to have the perception that they're part of a winning team, and so do you."

David replied, "I can take care of my staff. I just wanted you to know before this got out of hand."

David's facial expressions still didn't offer me the assurances his words did.

"Is there anything else we need to cover?"

David said, "No and thanks for giving me your time."

"You and your staff are all part of my team David. I'm always here for you. Thanks."

As I left David's office I wondered what kind of idiots I had hired to audit my books. I needed to find these guys and get their mouths shut. I could only hope that this meeting would be the end of this issue. You would think that one of the first things they would teach these auditor guys is confidentiality. I picked up my pace to the point of power walking, as I really needed to find some solace in the privacy of my office.

As I walked down the hall I heard Larry yell, "Rick, wait a minute." He ran up to me and said, "Let's have that meeting about sales this afternoon as a golf meeting, I can get us a 2 o'clock tee time at the club. I'd rather it was just you and I for this one. I need to ask you some things about Jim."

That's Larry. Everything can be solved if it's done on golf course. He has "Par" written on his forehead. To keep him motivated and to get me some time to think I replied, "Sounds good, set it up."

What really sounded good was any chance of getting away from this mess. I needed to motivate myself. I'm not good at details and everyone here was trying to give me more. I'm a result person and the result of this morning was a 2 o'clock tee time with Larry. I could see a vision of that tee box at 2. I was just about to open my office door as I said to Connie, "I've got some work to get done before lunch so hold all my calls."

Connie responded, "Jane's in your office. I tried to stop her."

I said, "And why is Jane in my office?"

Just then Jane stuck her head out and said, "Rick, I've been waiting for you. I couldn't find Larry so I've come to you for help. It's about my computer, it keeps saying "Don't you just love Eddie" and stuff like that. I can't get my work done and the guys in IT say it will be Wednesday before they can get to it. Rick, I'm trying to make sales for this company and I need my computer. Can you get these guys to help me now?"

"Did you put a request into helpdesk?"

"Rick, you know everything just gets lost in helpdesk. I really need your help getting this fixed now."

I must have had "I'll cause problems for myself" written on my forehead as I said, "Go by and tell Craig I said to bump you up on the list if he can. They've got a lot to do right now."

As she got to my door she turned and said, "Thanks. You look tired. Are you taking care of yourself? You'd better; you know we all depend on you so much."

I am tired. I don't know why but I had just gone around Craig's hallowed helpdesk… again. I'd hear from him on that I'm sure. Right now, I just don't care about that. I have to be able to use the systems here. This day just keeps getting better. At least Jane closed the door when she left. I wonder if anyone will notice if I turn out the lights and pretend to disappear?

No sooner had I begun to relax than Connie stuck her head in the doorway and said, "Joe's outside and says he has to talk to you about Eddie right now. I already told him you were tied up for the rest of today but he says he doesn't want to risk Eddie getting upset by any unfounded rumors."

"Send him in but tell him he gets 10 minutes and that's all."

Connie stated with a smile, "You got it."

Joe wasn't even through the door when he burst into his defense of Eddie. "Rick, we can't risk losing talented and dedicated people like Eddie just so Craig and those folks in IT can cover up their mistakes. Eddie could probably run our IT systems better than those guys. If he did go against any of our policies it was only because he was trying to help us."

I interrupted this regurgitation. "Relax, Joe. Eddie isn't going anywhere. He knows we all appreciate his efforts. Just tell him the current email problem is Craig's. Eddie doesn't need to do anything but focus on his work on the X-13 Product. Do you guys need my help to get this supply chain problem resolved?"

"No, I really think our suppliers are just stalling for time and that we will be fine in a couple of weeks."

"Why don't you and Eddie fly out and see what the problem is. You could fly out, see those folks on Friday and be back on Monday. Go over the changes in the new drawings while you're there. Denver is nice this time of year you know."

"Good idea, I'll send you an email, if I can, when I get it booked. We'll copy the new drawings to our notebooks rather than trust our email system. Thanks for your support. I know this will make Eddie feel better too. Thanks for your time."

"I know you'll get this done, Joe. Thanks." I actually felt good for the first time all day. My positive management skills had turned Joe's concern into a positive force as he and Eddie were going to get back on track. When I'm good, I'm really good. Just then my phone rang.

It was Connie. "I'm sorry, but Craig has called three times and says he has to see you this afternoon. Do you want me to keep him away from you?"

"Did he say what he needed?"

"Just that he has to see you."

"Tell him to come to my office in 20 minutes. I'll only have about 10 minutes for him."

Connie replied, "I'm sure he'll be here."

It seemed like only 20 seconds not 20 minutes when I heard Craig knocking at my door.

"Come on in Craig."

As he sat down I closed the door. The frustration was all over his face. That was better than some of the earlier visions I had seen on his forehead. "When do you want me to resign?"

"What?"

"You obviously don't understand what I'm trying to do, what I and my department have already done and without your support I'm wasting my time here."

"Craig, you need to calm down. You're part of our management team here and you do have my full support. This is a time for you to shine and show your skills in solving our current IT issues."

Craig's face was turning red as he continued with, "Where are you coming from? Were you in the same meeting I was just in? You left me hanging in the wind. You didn't support this company or me. I have fully explained over and over again how and why we have the problems with email that we have and your lack of support is undermining my credibility. You avoided the issues of violations of company policies and how we got in this mess to begin with. Is no one ever accountable around here? Someone needs to say, "Do it and do it the way I told you to." I know it's not politically correct but sometimes you just have to tell people what to do without getting their "buy-in". You don't want me around here."

"That's where you're wrong, Craig. Getting people to "buy-in" to your efforts is critical. If everyone isn't convinced of what we're doing and the methods we're using, we will not be successful. I've been in management longer than you and I know a bit about motivating people. You're going to have to trust me on this. If you give it time you will see it works."

"What about Eddie? Does he have any consequence for violating our policies and causing this mess?"

"I've already talked to Joe about Eddie."

Craig said, "And?"

"Let me make this clear. It's taken care of. Eddie's not a member of your department and not your concern. Now do you have any other concerns as to my support for you and your staff?"

"I don't believe you" was written all over his face as he continued with, "So you're telling me that Eddie is not going to cause us any more problems. At least this week."

"Eddie's not going to cause us problems. You know he brings a lot to this company. He's always here and always working on something."

"Eddie spends over half of his time here surfing adult web sites and the other half not finishing whatever he is supposedly working on."

"That's enough. I'm tired of people not working together."

Craig said, "I'm setting up at test for the email system and the "blacklist" issue on Friday. Just keep Eddie away from our computers."

"No problem. He will be out of town at our suppliers with Joe on Friday."

"You bribed them, didn't you? Rather than deal with this issue you gave them a trip. Don't you see what you're doing?"

"You're not doing yourself any favors with this attitude, Craig. I've supported you and the entire team. You need to show some positive management skills. I don't want you to say anything else. I want you to fix our systems and think about what you can do to help around here. I've got to go now so have a good lunch."

Craig started to speak, "I'm just…"

I interrupted with, "See you later, Craig and have a good lunch."

I noticed that my pace was very close to a slow jog as I left my office. "Connie, I'll be out the rest of the day. If you need me call on the cell phone."

"Sorry for all of the interruptions today. I'll try not to bother you this afternoon."

As I literally ran towards the parking lot I thought, lunch, I hope I can eat lunch. My stomach was turning inside out. So much for feeling good today. Craig was becoming a real problem. I have to get this email thing resolved. Until then I guess I will have to put up with him. Bribery; I'm not using bribery on anyone. Craig doesn't understand the positive approach I am using here. He's an old school disciplinarian type of management person. He really wants someone to be punished. I really don't know if Craig is going to continue to be a good fit around here. I wonder what has happened that has caused Craig to have such bad feelings towards Eddie. I tried moving on to more positive thoughts. I have lunch with my son and an afternoon of golf with Larry to look forward to. It's gotta be better than the events of the day so far.

Just then I ran into Jim." Be careful Rick. Where are you running to?"

"Sorry Jim. I'm glad I bumped into you. We can't get together this afternoon on those sales issues. I think we'll have to postpone until Thursday."

"Sorry to hear that. We really need to take a write off on some of the value of this inventory. It can save us on taxes. I really don't understand why we are holding so many inventory items anyway. Do you need me to talk to Larry about that? I don't think he understands what I said in the meeting."

I thought about the blanket orders Larry had insisted we needed to build up our business. The real result of those blanket orders was that we had ended up being our client's warehouse, at no risk or cost to them. Now that business was slow we were stuck with almost 3 years of inventory items. Rather than go into that mess with Jim right now I replied, "I understand we need to do something. We'll talk about it on Thursday. As for Larry, I'll be talking with him this afternoon. Thanks. Have a good lunch."

I jumped in my car as fast as I could and drove off. As I pulled up to my favorite restaurant I saw my son waiting for me on the patio. I had asked him to join me for lunch today so that I might help get him pumped up for the job interview he had this afternoon. Even though he graduated 3rd in his class, he still has some insecurity issues. I needed to help him any way I could. The last two interviews he had scheduled he hadn't even shown up for. At 24 years old he needed to get a job, get out of our house and get his life going. He didn't know it but a friend of mine is the CEO at the company he's applying at. If he shows up, he's got the job. As we talked over lunch I realized that he was going to bail on this opportunity if I didn't do something. As we were walking back to my car I said, "Listen, if you go for this interview today we will play golf on Saturday."

"Just you and me Dad?"

"Just you and I son, but you have to go for this interview. Trust me, you'll do great. Anybody would love to have you on their staff."

He said, "OK"

"Call me on my cell phone as soon as you're out of the interview."

As I headed back to the office, my thoughts wandered back to Craig's comments about bribery. Was that what I had just done with my son? Is that what I was doing with Larry and golf today? No. I'm a motivator and I see a bigger picture than Craig. As a matter of fact, Craig is a real challenge; he doesn't seem to be very motivated. He seems very defensive and closed to any ideas other than his. I've got to find a way to get him going in a different direction.

As I pulled into the parking lot Larry had the back of his BMW open and was doing something with his golf bag. I pulled in beside him and said, "Are you ready?"

With "PAR" still written across his forehead Larry smiled. "You know I am. It's really nice out today. Check out this new driver."

As I loaded my clubs into his car I did notice how nice a day it was. I hadn't noticed it before. That's not good. I need to find the harmony and peace so that I might be centered and appreciate the things around me.

On our drive to the club Larry denied me the peace I was seeking as he continued to talk. "What do you think about Jim? I know he's good at accounting but he doesn't really understand this business yet. I know a lot of our blanket orders have been canceled but the inventory we're holding will come in handy when the business comes back. We still have a ton of blanket orders on the books for the next two years. You and I have been through this before and we know the orders will come back soon. I really wish you'd talk to him about what he says in management meetings. I don't want to see him get embarrassed."

As he spoke I wondered if there were any two people left in this company that actually worked together. I need someone to help me hold this thing together. Larry doesn't have a clue as to what's going on. The only view he has is in the rear view mirror. He knows what happened in the past. He doesn't believe for a minute that his blanket orders and lack of a sales plan are hurting our company. He's just waiting for the past to return. I agreed that the business would return but I understood that we had to do whatever was needed to position ourselves to take advantage of the return. Larry didn't get that part. He just wanted to play golf and wait.

"Larry, we've got a huge tax bill which is due now. If we write off some of the cost of the inventory items we're holding we can save on our taxes. We need to cut our expenses any way we can right now."

"We don't need to cut our selling price though. We don't want to set precedent. We've never cut prices."

I said, "That's something we need to look at. If we can get the credit on the taxes and move at least 30% of the inventory within the next 60 days we can be here when the business picks back up."

"As always Rick, I'll do whatever you say but I don't think we should lower our prices."

As we pulled into the club parking lot I realized that I was done for the day. I needed to stop talking about business. Trying not to show the frustration I felt I said, "Larry, I just want to hit some balls. No more talk of business."

We had just gotten in our cart when my cell phone rang. I sat down in the cart and motioned for Larry to go first as I answered my phone. It was my friend who is the CEO at the company where my son had the interview today. I answered, "Hey bud, how did my son do? By the way thanks for helping us with this. I'm sure he'll do a great job for you."

He replied, "Sorry, Rick. I'm calling you to see where he is. He hasn't shown up."

I felt everything in my body slump. "I'm sorry. I'm sure something must have happened. I'll get back to you as soon as I can. Thank you very much for your help."

"No problem Rick. I hope everything is all right. We need to get together and play some golf."

"That sounds great. I'll call you tomorrow and we'll set up a time. Someone is ringing in so I've got to go for now."

As I clicked over to the incoming call I heard my son's voice. "I'm sorry Dad."

"Son you need to get over there and apologize to those people for being late to your interview. You can still…"

"Dad, I can't."

"What do you mean you can't? Get in your car and get over to that interview. I went out of my way to get this set up for you and you need to get over there now."

"Dad, I won't be going to the interview today. I'm in jail. This is my one phone call. Please come get me."

"Jail? What are you in jail for?"

"We should talk about it when you get here Dad."

"I want to know what you are in jail for."

"I bought some pot from a cop."

I just felt the bottom fall out of everything. What's happening to my life? There was a hole in the center of my body and the pain was incredible. "My god."

"I've got to get off the phone Dad. Are you going to come get me? We can talk when we get home."

"You're right about that son. We will talk when we get home. I'll be there as soon as I can. I'll call our lawyer. You need to just keep your mouth shut until I get there."

Larry was oblivious to my breakdown. "Come on Rick, You're up. I've already hit. It's great out here isn't it?"

I felt the tears rolling down my cheeks as the pain spread throughout my entire body. As I closed my eyes I began to have a vision. In this vision I am completely alone in a vast wasteland of grey colored mountains. Everything is grey, the sky, the trees, the rocks, everything. I am running. I'm running just as fast and as hard as I can. I am running away… far... far away.

ID10T Errors

1. Document management and the protection of your proprietary documents, products, concepts, etc.

Rick didn't seem to take notice of the security risk he was exposing his company to when he told Joe and Eddie to take the drawings for the new product on their laptops on their trip to the client's location. If he did take notice of any potential problems or risks he must have assumed that some mystical force in one of his visions was going to watch over his drawings as he gave no instructions or made any efforts to protect his company's property. In this story there was no mention by anyone as to whether these drawings would be password protected, saved on these laptops with some sophisticated encryption method or any mention of any concern for anything related to the protection of these proprietary drawings. This issue is a security concern. If this practice were done with some minimal concern for the security of these proprietary drawings this would have been fine. What would happen if the drawings and/or the laptops were stolen or accessed by someone other than Eddie and Joe? Given this company and these circumstances I think I would have emailed the drawings.

Simple procedures and policies as to how these proprietary items are stored, protected, shared, requested, used, etc. are standard operations for any successful organization.

Your company might find it has document management problems if you find your staff members are:

- Not sure where all of your documents are.
- Not sure who has requested the documents, why and for what purpose.
- Never quite sure if they are working with the current versions of files.
- Re-working overwritten revisions.

Document control, workflow, security, storage, and retrieval have all become much more complicated in today's workplace. For most people its complicated enough just keeping the files on their own computer organized. The complexity of these issues continues to escalate as collaborations across departments, locations and even companies becomes the normal method of doing business. There are tons of powerful document management system solutions available for document processes and enhanced productivity.

Typical solutions offered in these systems are:

- Streamlining document creation processes.
- Easy and secure retrieval, storage, usage.
- Controlling quality, policies and procedures.
- Structured workflow.

2. Loose Lips Sink Ships.

Rumors exist everywhere. The difference between how truth and rumors are received is usually based on a sound foundation of trust and communication. Trust is the best strainer in the world when it comes to finding the truth in a rumor. The people in this company no longer trust the company or each other. When the rumor that the company had financial difficulties began to circulate there wasn't a basis of trust to expel the fear that such a rumor can instill. The CEO attempted to address this issue with David, but with the environment he had created I doubt his attempts stopped any of the damage that these rumors were causing in his company. Do you think David felt any better after talking with Rick as to his concerns about the viability of the company? Rick never did answer David's original questions. He did give some vague explanations but nothing that would give David the security he was seeking. The lack of confidentiality exhibited by the auditors themselves was very unprofessional on their parts but might have been further evidence that this company did not always make its expectations clear. Talk about a security risk. You'd better watch the door if the most of the members of your company think the company is about to go bankrupt. There's no telling what will going out of those doors; people, skills, ideas, concepts, contacts, sales and more.

This situation could have easily been avoided had someone from our company gone over the expectations as well as the confidentiality agreement with the auditors before they began their work. Don't ever assume when you have the opportunity to clarify.

Rick doesn't understand that people need a complete set of standards.

- clear expectations and directions
- a structured environment
- boundaries
- rewards for compliance
- consequences for violations
- consistency

Rick uses some of these standards but not the complete set. He perceives some of these things as barriers to creativity. Rick's style was to find people with the skills to do the job and then get out of the way. The problem with that kind of management is that sometimes you don't get the results you expected. The clarity of the task is your responsibility when you hire someone. You have to take the steps to make sure that everyone involved has a clear understanding of everything involved. If you do these things you will get the job done and you will build trust and a basis for communication. When the expectations are met you offer rewards for compliance and accomplishment. If the expectations aren't met there must be consequences. Above all you must be consistent.

3. Visionaries do not equate to leaders and a leader is still needed here.

For all of the reasons I have mentioned earlier in this book, the lack of leadership in this company is still the number one security issue facing this company. Even when he takes off his wizard hat Rick has shown that he doesn't deal with issues, policies, procedures, details and even people very well. This company has no accountability and no real structure and Rick's actions indicate that he doesn't understand or even want these things. His methodology of positive management seems to have become a distorted form of bribery. There is a lack of willingness to face or resolve real issues. The only place it would seem that Rick's management efforts and visions have any chance of success are in the mystical land he creates in his own mind. Rick's visions may be more than just visions; they may be a sign of mental instability or flashbacks from earlier exposures to drugs. Who knows? Who cares? Rick and his visions are part of the problem. The lack of true leadership within this company has allowed everything to be turned inside out and upside down. Until such time as true leadership is found, this company will have to rely on luck, the parent company's deep pockets and products that sell themselves.

Wednesday

My name is Eddie. I'm an engineer and I'm very good at what I do. When you consider that I'm only 32 years old, it's amazing just how many things I can do. The entire engineering staff at this company had been working on the new product, X-13, for 2 years and just couldn't get it to work; they were stuck. That's why I was hired. In the year that I've been here, we've made tremendous progress on the product. I'm single and don't really have much of a social life. I spend at least 75 hours every week here at work. When I was in school I had the same dedication to the studies of my profession. Now that I'm in the corporate environment I am just as dedicated to the study of the game (the corporate structure and how it functions).

As I've worked here I've gotten to know the products, the company and the players in the company. When I say players I am referring to the people that play the corporate game. That's my perception of the corporate structure, management and co-workers. They're all players in the game. I play the corporate game and I intend to win. As luck would have it, I couldn't have found myself in an environment that offered me a better chance to win the game than here. There is no real leadership to contend with in this company. What we do have is a lot of little chiefs running around doing war dances. They spend more time fighting over territorial battles than getting their work done. They don't trust each other so they're easily manipulated. Rick, our CEO is the reason we have a lack of leadership around here. The guy is a nut. He claims to be a visionary and a motivator. You can lead him around like a puppy. All you have to do with him is plant some seeds, be politically correct and let him think it was his vision. When you're working with Rick you need to stay away from confrontation. You learn very quickly that his reaction to confrontation is very predictable. He will bribe you or run away. He won't deal with it. We have very little or no structure and no real accountability. It's the perfect environment for someone like me. I'm so good at what I do that my boss and his boss think that those 75 hours a week I spend here are completely filled with dedicated hard work. This place is ripe for a takeover and I just might be able move my career way beyond the position of engineer and I might do it in record time. If I can get a few select people to work with me I'll be running this place by the time I'm 34.

It's Wednesday morning around 8:30 and I'm sitting at my desk surfing the net at some of my favorite web sites. I absolutely love the responsiveness of the internet here at work. I've asked Joe, Rick and those folks in IT to get me hooked up with this kind of connection at home. So far I haven't been able to get that done. Just as I was about to get interested in one of the web sites I was surfing, Jerry Jumper came bursting into my office. My focus was to quickly shift my computer away from the website and on to a screen burn mode as I looked at Jerry and said, "What are you doing here this time of day? You look like somebody just stole your beamer. Are you OK?"

"No, I'm not OK. Do I look like I'm OK? I've got a mess on my hands and if I can't clean it up or do something I could lose my job."

"Calm down Jerry. Don't worry about getting fired. Think about where you are. Nobody ever gets fired from here. What is the problem?"

"I was on line checking the bill for my company credit card for last month. I normally do that so I can get a jump on my report. The bill is $40,000.00!!!" Jerry's stress was evident from the huge bulges in his forehead and neck as he continued with, "That's $40,000.00 for last month. I never spent $40,000.00. Larry's going to kill me. I didn't do this. I don't know what is going on. Somebody's got to fix this. Rick's gonna kill me. Man, did I get into a mess this time!"

I asked, "Have you called the credit card company yet? Have you asked about the bill and any of the details?"

"I can't pay that bill. Do you think Larry will try to make me pay it? My wife is going to kill me. What am I gonna do?"

"Jerry you need to calm down and listen."

Realizing that he was very upset and hadn't heard what I'd just asked him I repeated, "Have you called the credit card company yet? Have you asked about the bill and any of the details?"

Jerry replied, "No, I was too upset. The site is still up on my screen in my office. I just came in here."

"I'll bet you haven't even looked at the details yet to see if all of the charges are the correct amounts. Did you check to see if all of the charges were even at places that you've been to?"

"I knew you'd give me some help, Eddie. No I haven't done any of those things but does it really matter? No matter what they say I didn't put $40,000.00 worth of charges on that credit card last month. Do we have to pay it?"

"I can't tell you anything about what anybody has to pay until we get into the details. What I can tell you is that you need to relax. First of all you don't have to worry about Larry. He's not going to do anything. He needs you. If we handle this right, Rick won't kill you, he'll give you a trip as a reward for fixing the problem; that's if we decide to let him know it ever existed at all. Let's go to your office, print out the bill and start going over the details. After we see what's what we can call the credit card company and see what is going on."

Jerry was obviously still upset as he repeated his position again. "I don't care what they say I'm not going to pay them or anybody else $40,000.00. I can't."

"Calm down and listen."

Jerry seemed to have finally understood that there might be a way out of this. I was trying to help and he did show some visible signs of relief when he responded, "Thanks."

I asked, "Who else knows about this?"

Jerry replied, "Nobody. I came straight to you."

"Good. Just let me get my computer system to a stopping point. I was in the middle of something when you walked in and I don't want to lose any work." I opened my internet browser, erased the history for today and then closed the browser on my computer. "Let's go see what you've done, buddy."

Before we left my office I asked Jerry to wipe off his face as he was dripping with sweat. I guess he never heard the phrase "never let them see you sweat." As I handed him a tissue I realized that this guy had come very close to losing it this morning. I now had the opportunity to have him very indebted to me once again. I thought to myself, "I am very good at this game." Isn't it funny how things just fall in your lap sometimes? As we headed to Jerry's office he finally began to calm down, which was good. We didn't need anyone else getting wind of this situation. Right now we needed to see what we were actually dealing with. As we walked, I thought about who Jerry Jumper was.

Jerry Jumper is a pretty boy who probably takes longer to get ready than his wife. He's one of those people you wish you could buy for what they're worth and then sell them for what they think they're worth. Arrogant, isn't he? Everyone pampers him. If he can't get the attention of every female in the room, he somehow feels denied. He's very much into the right clothes, the right school, the right car, the right clubs and basically right up his bosses butt. He doesn't like his boss or our CEO, Rick. He does know enough about the game to keep them both on his side. Jerry Jumper is our lead salesman. That is to say he has more sales than anyone else in the company. His main sales account happens to be one of our parent companies and represents well over 75% of our total sales for the entire company. If you talked to Jerry about what he has done here, you'd think he had developed that account and the relationship from scratch. Like most of his business accomplishments that account was handed to Jerry on a silver platter. Jerry and I do have some things in common as we do visit some of the same websites and watering holes. He's married and has two kids but is really just a kid himself. I personally wouldn't describe him as a salesman. He's a reactionary not a planner, a glorified order taker with a little bit of style. He has a part to play in the corporate moves that I plan to make in this company. I could trust Jerry. I certainly wouldn't be putting the trust in him that I have if I didn't have so much on him. The stories I could tell about Jerry would definitely not help his professional or his personal life. One of the corporate rules I had already learned very well was "what happens on the road stays on the road". Jerry is an ally and a friend of mine, at least in my efforts to take over this company.

As we headed towards Jerry's office, I noticed that Joe was coming right towards us. Since he's currently my boss I have to acknowledge him so I said, "Good morning Joe."

"Good news Eddie. We're going to see the suppliers on Friday. Our flight is at 9:00 AM and we'll return Monday at 4:30. We've got a meeting Friday afternoon and then we'll have the weekend in Denver. You've never been there have you?"

"No I haven't Joe. How'd you arrange this? I thought we were cutting back on travel."

"I convinced Rick that we had to show those guys the changes in drawings in person. I told him they would never understand what we really wanted if we couldn't get face to face with them. Make sure you download a copy of the drawings onto you laptop."

I couldn't help but smile as I said, "Sounds great. I'll be ready."

Joe looked at Jerry and said, "Are you OK Jerry? You look like you don't feel to well."

"I'm OK Joe. It was just a long night last night. The kids have got some sort of bug and it kept everyone up half the night."

"Been there done that. Hope everyone gets better. See you guys later."

Jerry and I both said, "Later Joe."

As we entered Jerry's office I could see the credit card information was still up on his computer screen. I sat down at his computer, sent the output of the details of the bill to the printer and started to look over the list of charges on the screen while we waited for the hard copy. There were a series of 8 charges over a five-day period to the same place of business that totaled around $33,000.00 that immediately got my attention. The fact that there were charges from a dance club that Jerry and I had been to before caused me to smile as I asked, "Did you enjoy your trips to the dance club last month? Do you get some sort of special treatment for this kind of money? If you didn't you should have."

Jerry responded defensively saying, "What are you talking about? It was just the usual sort of thing. Our clients wanted to go. I've been there before; it's no big deal. You've been there with me. You know what happens there. What's the big deal?"

I couldn't help it as I laughed out loud. "I've been there with you but I've never gone there 5 days in a row and I never spent $33,000.00 there. I don't think I know just what goes on for that kind of money."

"Shut up Eddie. This is serious and I need your help."

"Was there someone there you particularly liked or do you get group rates for this kind of cash? Do you get some special dances or services for that kind of money? I'll bet they'll remember you the next time you walk in the door."

As he walked around the desk to look at the screen his hands were shaking. "You are full if it Eddie. Show me these charges. I went to that stupid club one time last month and maybe spent $1,200.00 to

$1,400.00." His eyes continued to scan the computer screen as he read the charges I had just mentioned. The aggravation was evident in his voice as he continued, "These are crap. I was there one day. I wasn't there any of those other days. I didn't make these charges. What's going on? This is a mistake."

"I don't know for sure yet, but if you're telling me these charges aren't charges that you've made on this card than we may have a case of credit card fraud or identity theft."

Jerry looked puzzled as he asked, "What?"

"It looks like somebody has your credit card numbers and they're making charges on the card. I hope this is the only card involved. Think, Jerry. I need you to remember as much as you can here. Are you getting any strange charges on any other credit cards?"

"Remember what man? Are you kidding me? How does something like that happen?"

I asked, "Do you still have the company card?"

As he looked in his wallet to see if the card was there Jerry said, "Of course I do."

"Somebody has made these charges. They could have made a copy of the numbers, gotten a duplicate receipt or a copy of a bill. It really doesn't matter now. What matters now is we have to get a halt on any new charges and get these old charges cleared up."

Jerry said, "How do we do that?"

I said, "First let's call the credit card company and get them to issue a new card or at least put a hold on this card so no new charges can occur. You and I need to go over every line on this bill to verify which lines are the charges that you actually made. We'll call the credit card company back and see where we are after that. There could be other charges that haven't gotten posted so don't be surprised if what we've found isn't all that's out there. You need to check on any other cards you have."

Jerry picked up the hard copy from the printer and we began to go over each and every line of the bill. My thoughts began to wander as to how Jerry was going to pay me back for getting him through this mess. It didn't take me long as I knew he was going to Larry's house for lunch today. I asked, "Are you going to Larry's house for lunch today?"

Jerry said, "Yeah, why?"

"I need you to go to his home computer and turn off the anti virus protection software. It's keeping me from accessing his computer from here and I need to do some maintenance on his system. I don't have time to run out there or I'd do it myself."

Jerry said, "I'd be glad to if I knew how. Do you really need it done today?"

"I'll show you how on your machine. It's easy. I really do need it done today. Will you?"

"Sure Eddie, I'll be glad to help you any way I can."

After we finished going over the credit card bills and called the credit card company, I showed Jerry how to turn off the anti virus software on his computer. He said he felt comfortable and could do it on Larry's home computer. He said it should be done no later than 2:00 this afternoon. Good thing he hadn't read his emails from IT or listened any of the times Craig had explained about our anti virus protection and our current email issues or he would have figured out that I was up to something. He was too busy being thankful that he didn't have to pay $40,000.00 out of his pocket. It had been a great start to the day. As I got up to head back to my office Jerry said, "Thanks a lot Eddie. You really helped me out here."

I replied with a smile, "No problem. Just glad I could help." I reminded Jerry that we weren't done yet as I continued with, "We've got some work to do here and we need to get it done quickly. You need to check the bills on every other credit card you have. You can do it online. Call me if you see any strange charges on any of your other cards."

As I walked back to my office I thought about how Craig had been on my back lately. I guess he'll be a little too busy to bother me when 500 to 1000 bogus emails start flying out of Larry's home computer again. I wonder how he'll explain that? A lot of people around here already doubt that he or his staff can keep our systems running. This is too easy. I may be running that IT department sooner than I planned. All I have to do is wait.

To my surprise my office door was open and there sat Jane in all her glory. In most environments she would be way out of my league but not here. She works here so she's around all the time. It's not like she has a choice. I am slowly getting her to have some sort of reliance on me, a confidence in me, and respect for me. I have been building the basis for a relationship one step at a time. In the corporate environment, you don't have to look like Jerry to get your foot in the door with a woman; just be patient. I learned a long time ago that women are attracted to power and money. I didn't have either, yet, but to anyone paying attention, I definitely look like someone who is on the fast track to bigger and better things. Jane's a bright girl and I'm sure she's already noticed my potential around here. Maybe that's why she's sitting in my office. She interrupted my fantasy as she said, "Eddie, I need your help."

"What can I do for you?"

She said, "It's about my computer, it keeps saying "don't you just love Eddie" and stuff like that. I can't get my work done and the guys in IT say it will be Wednesday before they can get to it. Eddie, I need your help. I know the guys in IT probably did this just because you helped me with my software before. You know I'm trying to make sales for this company and I need my computer. Can you help me now?"

"Those guys in IT are nuts. Jane, I'm really sorry you had a problem. I'll come with you right now and see what I can do for you."

As we walked towards her office I couldn't imagine how this day could go any better. Jane was beginning to come to me for help on a regular basis. I was going to save her again. If we were in a bar this girl wouldn't give me the time of day, but here we were and she was the one who came looking for me. I am good. As I sat down at her computer she started filing some papers. After I quit wasting time watching her file papers, I emailed myself the file that caused the pop-ups and then erased it from her system. Another 15 minutes or so of chitchat and then I informed her that I had fixed her computer. It wasn't going to pop up with "don't you just love Eddie" anymore. I couldn't resist it when I laughed and said, "Jane, don't you just love Eddie now?"

She smiled as I got up to leave. "You're so funny. You're the best Eddie. You get more stuff done for me than anyone around here. I'm so thankful you're here. Now maybe I can get some work done. Thanks so much. Let me know if I can ever help you."

As I headed back to my office I thought, this day just keeps getting better. Jerry and Jane are in my pocket, I'm going to Denver for the weekend and there is going to be a huge security hole in our email system. The fact that Jerry was going to get Larry's virus protection turned off gave me great cause for optimism. Larry's kids will get online and have his system infected with the email virus all over again within 2 hours. Larry's home system will begin to flood our network and our client's networks with 500 to 1000 SPAM messages by early Thursday morning at the very latest. It seems Craig and his staff members are going to continue to have difficulty solving our email problems. I'm not sure they'll ever get this fixed.

If Craig tries to tie me into this mess or put any of the blame on me he'll just dig himself a deeper hole with Rick and Joe. Craig is on everybody's nerves right now. He really doesn't need to be associated with any negative issues. He doesn't get that but I do. It's all in the timing. I may be running the IT department sooner than I had planned. I hope so cause I'm bored with this X-13 thing. It just doesn't excite me. I need to be stimulated.

Back in my office, I sat down at my desk and checked my database of user names and passwords. I needed to make sure that the passwords I had just used for Jerry and Jane were up to date in my files. I had about 25 of our staff members' user names and passwords on file. After I updated the file I started to read through my emails. Just then I caught a glimpse of Joe standing at my door. "Joe, what can I do for you?"

As he pulled the door to my office closed I realized he was actually concerned over whatever it was he was about to say. "I need to talk to you about how we're working with Craig and the folks in IT."

Trying to give him the assurance that I thought he was seeking I replied, "We're working together just fine aren't we? I know my efforts to help got misinterpreted but I thought I had cleared that up with Craig. A lot of people around here ask me to help on their computers because they know that I know what I'm doing. I thought I'd made it clear to everyone that I was here to help. I don't want to cause you or anybody here problems. You know I'll do whatever you need Joe. What can I do to help get things back on track?"

"I probably shouldn't say this but if I were you I'd want to know. I just came out of meeting where Craig went off on the fact that you had caused the email problems and that you went against our company policies. He wants you to stay out of IT issues all together."

"I didn't cause any problems. Craig's own emails and the emails from his staff say that this mess is because of a virus. I didn't create the virus and I sure didn't bring it into our systems. The only thing I've ever done around here is try to help. If his staff would take care of the people around here maybe everyone wouldn't feel the need come to me for help."

"Rick and I support your efforts here. Everyone that was at that meeting understands that you are appreciated around here. The only thing I want you to do is not to get involved with any IT issues for a while. If someone comes to you for help on any IT issues tell them to go through IT. Let them give Craig and his staff their problems."

"What if IT doesn't get things done? You know a lot of people around here say that if you want to get something buried just send it to helpdesk. There's a reason people started asking me for help in the first place. Don't those attitudes say something to management around here?"

"That's exactly the point here, Eddie. It's time for IT to be responsible for what does or doesn't get done in their department. I know all of your efforts were well intended. I wish we could work with these folks in IT but this is the way it is for now. I'm supporting you, Eddie. I even told Rick that I thought you could probably run that department better than Craig."

I thought to myself, that's just the type of endorsement that I'm looking for. That department could be mine any day now. You never know what type of pressures might occur to force a sudden change. Pressures like reoccurring holes in your email system. "Thanks for your support. I'm sure everyone in IT is working hard to get things done around here. By the way have you heard anything about when I can expect to have high speed hook up at home? I'm still putting in a lot of hours here and it'd save me a lot of time if I could work at home. I sent the request into helpdesk 4 or 5 weeks ago."

"I'll talk to Craig about it again. I don't know what the hold up is. I've asked him about it twice already. I'm sorry. I know you put in more hours than anybody here. You shouldn't have to work all of those extra hours."

"I don't care about the amount the hours. I just want to make the best use of my time. I really need that connection. I know you're doing everything you can for me. On another subject, a friend of mine lives out in Denver and I thought we could get together while we're there."

"That would be great Eddie. I think we can get tickets to see a ballgame while we're there. Why don't we meet at the game?"

"Sounds good. I'll get in touch my friend. We could grab a bite to eat after the game."

"See you later Eddie. Thanks for all you're doing around here."

Joe and Rick just jumped into my pocket along with Jerry and Jane. I hope it isn't getting crowded in there. It's always good to have people supporting you.

As I leaned back in my chair, I heard my phone ring. My friend Jake was on the line. "When are you going to let me buy some more memory sticks? I need 2 sticks right now if you've got them." Jake ran his own computer business. We had helped each other on all kinds of things.

I had been buying and installing memory in the computers in our department for about six months now. I had replaced some memory in some of the computers and had been selling some of the old memory sticks that I had taken out of those computers to Jake.

I still had about 8 sticks left so I said, "Anytime you want it buddy. I've got 8 sticks left. You ought to take it all as I don't know if I can ever let you have it this cheap again."

"I'll take it all. Why don't you meet me for lunch and I'll get it from you then."

"Meet you at the watering hole at 12:00."

I've got this place wired. I was going to put some extra cash in my pocket. The company was just going to throw those old memory sticks away anyway. Somebody ought to benefit from their use. That somebody might as well be me.

It was about 11:30 so I finished checking my emails and then shut down my system. With a smile on my face, a bounce in my walk and memory sticks in my pocket I headed out the door to lunch. I was hungry and lunch at my favorite watering hole was just what I needed.

As I pulled out of the parking lot I saw Craig and some of his staff getting into Craig's car. I wondered if I would keep any of those folks on staff when I take over that department. Out of that group, who could I count on as part of my team?

Jake's face lit up as I walked into the restaurant. The deal we had going on these memory sticks was just the tip of the iceberg. Little did he know how soon I might be in charge of the IT department? We had talked about my career moving in that direction but Jake didn't know about the current developments. "Eddie, over here, I've got us a table and your hot wings are on the way."

I smiled as I sat down at the table. "Jake, we've got a lot to talk about. I might be taking over as head of the IT department very soon."

"Are you kidding? Is Craig quitting?"

"Craig may not have much to say about it. He's been digging himself a big hole with Rick and most of the management team. If he doesn't get things cleaned up soon he might as well jump in that hole." I laughed as I said, "He just doesn't know how to play or work well with others."

"I'd love to see you in charge over there. Maybe if you take over I can get some business with you guys. Craig cut me out of the loop when he took over. I used to do a lot of work on your systems."

"You've done a lot of good work for us. If I get this position I'll be relying on you a lot. Don't let me down. Here's the memory you ask for."

"Here's your cash. Is that all of the memory you've got left?"

"What else do you need? I can probably come up with something."

About that time the wings showed up and Jake and I feasted, plotted, planned and laughed for the next hour. It was time to get back to my office when I said, "Call me on Monday. I'll send you a post card from Denver."

"And just why are you getting to go to Denver?"

"Business. I doubt I'll get to see or do anything else while I'm there."

Jake laughed and said, "Yeah, right. You've got it made. Talk to you on Monday."

It was 1:55 when I got back to the office so I went straight into to my 2 o'clock meeting with Joe, David and Rick. We were going to go over the changes in our product drawing that Joe and I were taking to Denver. I was feeling great. The atmosphere in the room was full of excitement over our new changes to the product, the teamwork we were sharing and the anticipation of the new sales this product was going to generate. I was getting a lot of praise, as if I had been the one that had actually made the changes that were going to finally get this product working. Rick was beaming as he said, "Eddie if this works out we've got to bring you back from Denver and let everyone know just what you've done for us all. I know Joe and all the members of his entire team are proud of you."

"That's an understatement Rick. This guy puts in more hours and works harder than anyone I've ever been around. Do you know he's here at his desk 75 hours a week? We need to get him a high speed hook up at home so he could work from home."

"Consider it done. Have you put in a request with Craig?"

"Don't get me started on that guy. I've put in several requests to get Eddie hooked up at home and nothing gets done. Everything gets lost in helpdesk."

"I'll put the request in myself. Eddie, you'll have high speed hook up next week at the latest."

I smiled as I said, "Thanks, Rick. It will help a lot. I just hope these new changes fix our problems. I know how important it is that we get this thing to market. We all know how badly we need to get some new sales going."

All of the sudden the door flew open with such a force that it slammed against the wall and almost knocked the clock to the floor. When everything quit shaking, I noticed that Craig was there, standing in the doorway. His eyes were full of rage, everything about his body language said "back off". As he started to speak, I realized that I was probably going to be running IT very soon.

"I'm glad the three of you are all together. It'll save me a lot of time. Eddie, it looks like you've got Larry's home computer going crazy again. It's sending out emails everywhere and they're all contaminated with the virus. Joe, you haven't done a thing to stop this have you? As for you Rick, you tell me to fix something and then you won't help me or let me fix it. You fix it Rick. Fix it right now. Fire Eddie!"

Rick looked like a deer caught in the headlights of a car; he wasn't about to move, speak or do anything. He was in shock. Joe, on the other hand, looked as if he was about ready to go in for some hand-to-hand combat. Realizing that I could possibly stop a murder and score some points by showing some leadership skills, I quickly and firmly stated, "Craig, let me assure you that I had nothing to do with Larry's computer or your problems. As you can see we're having a meeting right now. I'm not sure what has caused your current problem but maybe we can talk about it when you calm down."

"Shut up Eddie. You think you've got everyone here tricked into thinking you're some kind of company man, with great ideas and good work ethics. I know how much time you spend working and how much time you spend on your American Sexual Services web site. You don't fool me, you're a…"

I interrupted before he had a chance to say anything else about my activities here at work. "I don't have to listen to this kind of crap from you. You can't even keep our systems working. You might think you've found someone to blame your problems on, but you haven't. Pick on someone else. I won't be your scapegoat. Why don't you just go fix our email and quit acting like an idiot?"

While I was speaking Joe had jumped to his feet and was moving towards Craig when he said, "You need some help leaving the room Craig? I've had enough. I'd be glad to help you out that door."

"Are you just going to sit there? I'm telling you the truth and I'm doing what you hired me to do. Are you going to do anything Rick?"

"Everybody just stop talking! Go to your office Craig. I'll be there just as soon as I finish here."

Craig's eyes were bulging, the veins in his neck were exploding and the sweat was beginning to pour, "Is Eddie fired or not?"

"I said go to your office, and I mean right now. I'll discuss these issues with you later. I don't want to hear anything else from anyone. I mean it. GO!"

Craig slammed the door with such a force as to cause the clock to fall and break into ten different pieces as it hit the floor. That was a really nice clock. "Rick, you've got to put a leash on Craig. He's out of control. If Larry's computer is having email problems again it's probably because it was never really fixed. This is just more evidence that Craig and his staff aren't getting the job done around here. You and I both know Eddie didn't have anything to do with it."

The awkward circumstances of this incident were obviously making it difficult for Rick to speak as he said, "Craig is having some difficulties right now. I do apologize to the two of you for his unprofessional interruption and his outburst. I don't know what we will have to do to get this resolved but I certainly hope I can count on the two of you."

In an effort to score more points and reassure Rick that everything would be OK, I smiled and said, "You know we're part of your team Rick. We'll do whatever it takes to make this work. You certainly don't have to apologize for Craig. Joe and I just hope he can get control of things."

Joe added, "He needs to get control of something."

For the next 15 minutes or so we wrapped up our thoughts on the changes in the drawings and our trip to Denver. There were mixed emotions as we left the meeting. I left the meeting feeling great. Rick left with a confused look on his face and an obvious burden in his heart. Joe was just starting to come off of combat mode.

As we walked down the hall I said, "Thanks for your support in there. Don't let that guy upset you. He's digging his way right out of a job."

"I'm just giving you the support you deserve, Eddie. Craig just lost all of my respect and trust. He can't even keep the systems running. What are we paying that guy for? Rick needs to get him out of here."

As I opened the door to my office and started inside I said, "See you later. Thanks again, Joe."

Sitting down at my desk I realized that I couldn't have scripted today's events any better than what had actually occurred. I felt like dancing.

Just then I heard my door open and saw Rick's worried face. "Eddie I want you to take the rest of today off. Go on home early for a change."

"That's nice of you, Rick, but I've got some things I need to get done."

"Eddie, you need to listen to me and just go on home."

"Am I in some kind of trouble?"

"It's Craig I'm worried about, Eddie. I don't want him to bother you and I just don't know what he's going to do."

"I can take care of him. You don't have to worry about that."

"I want you to do me a favor and do what I ask, Eddie."

"OK"

It took me about 15 minutes to get to a point where I could wrap things up and leave for the day. I had called Jake and we were going to get together and have a drink. I could only hope that I could enjoy the evening as much as I had the day.

As I walked by Rick's office on my way to my car I heard Craig's voice. "Why am I in here talking to you? Where's Eddie? You gave him the rest of the day off didn't you? What's wrong with you?" I guess Craig wasn't having as good a day as I was.

ID10T Errors

1. Credit fraud, unauthorized charges and Identity theft.

Credit fraud and unauthorized charges involve the theft of your credit card or account number. Although protection from substantial financial loss to the cardholder normally does exist, these types of activities may have adverse effects on your credit. You might be charged higher interest rates, have loan request refused and you could jeopardize your ability to obtain further credit. These types of activities may also be just be the beginning of identity theft. Identity theft is when someone assumes your identity, opens bank, credit card or other accounts to commit fraud, theft and run up all sorts of bad debt in your name without you ever knowing. Victims of the crime of identity theft have been arrested, had their driver's license revoked, lost pay, lost jobs and worse.

A conservative estimate would be that there are more than 500,000 new cases of identity theft each year. There were potentially 8 million victims when hackers were able to view 8 million credit card numbers in the system of an Omaha-based processing company Data Processors International. Another 55,000 identities were compromised when a hacker broke into the system at University of Texas. That hacker gained access to Social Security numbers, e-mail addresses, students, former students and employee's names. We can't sit and wait until legislation is passed that truly protects us from identity theft. We must take control of our personal information, be vigilant and speak up.

In our story Eddie referred to Jerry's credit card fraud as identity theft. Jerry's situation actually involves theft, credit card fraud and possibly identity theft. If you have any concerns over unauthorized charges, credit fraud or identity theft, get copies of your current credit card bills and your credit report. Your current bills will allow you to verify the current charges and your credit report will show you if there are accounts listed or charges made that you haven't opened or that you shouldn't be held responsible for. Some of the details involved with your identity are out of your control, but it is your responsibility to do your best to try to protect yourself.

Suggestions for protecting your identity:

- When you make a charge with a credit card, be aware of how the transaction itself occurs. Make sure copies of your credit card transaction and your card number are protected. Never give your credit card number or personal information to anyone you do not know and never over the phone.
- Monitor your credit report. It contains your SSN, present and prior employers, a listing of all account numbers, and your overall credit score.
- Subscribe to a credit monitoring service that will notify you whenever someone uses your name.
- Mail bill payments from the post office.
- Do not carry extra credit cards or other identity documents except when needed.
- Cancel unused credit cards and checking accounts.
- Verify every single charge on your credit card statements before paying them.
- Maintain copies of your license and credit cards so you have all the account numbers, expiration dates and phone numbers in case they are lost or stolen.
- Shred all old bank, credit card and credit statements and "junk mail". Guard your Social Security number. Do not print your Social Security number on your checks.

Jerry not only committed a careless act, he committed a crime of theft. By not properly caring for the company credit card he could be viewed as committing theft and be required to repay the amount of the charges. He is liable for those charges. It would be my guess that our character Jerry wasn't very concerned or careful as he made charges at the "dance club". I'm sure that he will continue to deny any wrongdoing. One needs to always be aware of one's surroundings. I'm not sure Jerry should trust everyone he meets when he travels and it is not in our company's best interest to continue to trust Jerry with a credit card.

In his efforts to help Jerry it may have seemed that Eddie was very helpful. He did get Jerry to attempt to verify the current charges on his credit card bill. Eddie didn't get a credit report for the company or for Jerry. The risk that there are other accounts out there that Jerry hasn't opened is not being addressed. The company and Jerry are still at risk and will remain at risk until all of these issues are addressed. Jerry needs to learn to take control of and to protect his company's and his own personal information. If he doesn't, he will continue to be a huge security risk to his company and himself.

2. Property Theft.

Corporate theft is a grave abuse of trust. There is no basis of trust within this company. The crimes of theft that Eddie has committed are unfortunately not that unusual. Greedy or disgruntled employees commit most corporate crimes. Theft of goods, embezzlement, unauthorized use of services, abuse of credit cards and expense accounts are the most common crimes. Given the environment that Eddie works in, it is not surprising that the sabotage of corporate infrastructure is also occurring. It's only a matter of time before crimes such as the sale of trade secrets or products occur.

Never underestimate good old-fashioned property theft. It is still a major security concern. When Eddie upgraded the memory components on some of his department's computers, he took the old memory and sold it. No one seemed to even notice except for Eddie's friend Jake who was Eddie's partner in crime. Eddie verbalized that the company would have just thrown the old memory away. If he truly had good intentions towards his company he might have suggested that the company see if other systems within the company could use the memory or if there was a resell market. Eddie's crime may seem to be small in the scale of things but his actions will lead him into more serious acts of criminal behavior.

One of the best ways to avoid theft is to build and maintain an atmosphere of value and trust.

Management must offer:

- clear definitions of expectations
- rewards and consequences
- value
- teamwork and ownership
- a consistent approach

Together these actions will build a basis for an environment of value and trust. If you don't value and trust each other, you will not value or trust what each of you do.

Some more specific methods to help avoid theft and maintain an environment of value and trust are:

- the use of standard procedures and policies
- inventory control
- asset and supply chain management

If you don't know what you have, it's almost impossible to know if something is missing.

Corporate management must also offer an environment with standard policies and procedures as to:

- accountability
- procurement functions
- installation of equipment (hardware and software etc.)
- proper maintenance
- replacements
- upgrades
- life cycle costs

The lack of these made for tremendous opportunities for theft and fraud in our company.

It would be wonderful if every employee were:

- self motivated
- took pride in a job well done
- felt trusted
- was driven to do the very best job possible
- was valued as a member of the team

- trusted in his company
- shared the responsibility to be an effective employee

Unfortunately there is a small percentage of the management and staff in our story that seems more inclined to be motivated by greed and self-indulgence. Not a good mixture for success.

3. Corporate sabotage and SPAM.

PC viruses accounted for an estimated $35 billion in global business losses in 2003 alone. Eddie has committed corporate sabotage in efforts to damage Craig's career and further his own. He has shown blatant disregard for anyone and anything other than himself. The lack of structure, accountability, knowledge and the general chaos that is rampant in this company have allowed Eddie the opportunity to play his destructive games.

Every time Eddie turns off the virus protection on any of the computers attached to the network, he exposes his entire company to potential disaster. It's hard to imagine a more malicious act. The earlier statement of 35 billion dollars is a very conservative estimate of the cost to businesses globally related to spam and viruses. The economic and financial impact of attacks such as spam threats and network viruses continues to climb.

The attack in our story started with a home computer system that could connect to the company's network remotely. It became infected with a spam-generating virus. That virus then caused a surge in the company's network traffic as well as the company's client's network traffic. This prompted the network administrators of our client's in Germany to block all e-mail coming from our company. Our company was on a "Blacklist".

The threat of spam and virus attacks has become more than just a nuisance and is increasing exponentially. Any business that is not addressing these issues will likely become a victim.

Craig and his staff had made attempts to address these security issues with normal password protection schemes, policies, procedures, constant monitoring and virus protection schemes. As is evidenced in our story, these efforts are useless without the management support and the enforcement needed to succeed. The implementation of such protection measures can only be effective and some level of security accomplished with the full support of an entire organization. It has to start at the top and filter all the way down. If this company doesn't begin to seriously address these issues the clock is ticking and the bomb will go off. It's just a matter of how big a bomb it is and when does it explode. It looks like Eddie is hoping for Thursday.

Suggestions as to how you should respond in the event of such an attack:

- Document everything relating to the incident.
- Limit the damage as much as possible. Identify, isolate and stop the attack.
- Repair the damage.
- Implement the solution.
- Make sure that the system is running normally.
- Determine how the incident occurred and how it can be prevented in the future.
- Increase monitoring, assess your results, review your policies, procedures, protection schemes, personnel, support systems, management, hardware and software.
- Learn.

Thursday

As I sat at my desk I continued my search to find the most qualified consultants to help our company meet some of our future engineering needs. With our current rate of sales it was obvious that we had to cut back on our staff. I was searching for a team of professionals that would be available a on project-by-project basis to replace some of our full time staff members. Rick has asked me to help him find these replacements so that we can cut our payroll expenses. I was getting blurry eyed looking through the maze of standardized bids, responses, brochures and performance reviews. I thought about the people we were going to lose. How was this going to affect their families? I know it would be a terrible hardship for my family to bear. As I continued with my efforts, I found it difficult to find an easy "apples-to-apples" comparison from the over 20,000+ consultants available. My mind was full of all sorts of doubts and questions about what I was being asked to do. Where did those 20,000+ consultants come from? Where is their loyalty? What about the security risk of outsourcing these services? Are there any controls we ought to have in place prior to getting involved with this kind of thing? Everywhere I look, I see companies sending jobs somewhere else. With outsourcing aren't we exporting one of our base industries—the knowledge industry? Why did Rick dump this on me? When is my job going to be outsourced?

Some say that outsourcing is a product of globalization and is inevitable. Outsourcing decisions that are based solely on cost will surely find that every job can be done cheaper in some country where there is a huge disparity in wages. You get what you pay for and we are heading towards a disaster in the long run. The money that will be saved now will ultimately be spent fixing disasters that will surely occur in the future. Decisions should not be based on short-term cost benefits alone. Sometimes part of the cost of success is long-term investment. What are we doing?

My name is David and I am a 34-year-old part time National Guard member, husband, father of 2 boys and the VP of Manufacturing. I've worked with some of the folks around here for over 20 years if you count our time working together at our parent companies. Rick and I have worked together longer than anyone here. There was a time when I could count on and believe in him. Unfortunately that's not the case now. Rick has turned into the invisible man. He has abandoned us all as he runs from his responsibilities. I have voiced my concerns about the issues we are facing only to feel that he doesn't want to hear or deal with them. He knows that these issues are destroying this company. He really thinks that our parent companies will save us. He's not even taking the responsibility for his own job performance. My greatest fear with Rick is that he's lost himself. It's happened at a time when we desperately need him.

I tried to get back on track as I checked to see if I had correctly stated our needs, requirements, estimates, budgets and timelines in my presentation to the vendors. I was just trying to focus on something other than Rick and the issues here. I had already checked all of these at least 5 times this morning. I really don't like the feel of what I'm doing around here lately. Its 8:30 in the morning and I already need a break.

"David, do you have a minute?"

I looked up to see Craig standing in the doorway to my office. My first thought was great I'll talk with Craig and get that break that I need. I became a bit concerned when I saw how stressed Craig looked. He was sweating, his voice was cracking and his hands were shaky. "Come on in Craig. I've got about 15 minutes I can give you."

"Did you get a chance to read the email I sent out to everyone this morning?"

"I've been so tied up I haven't even looked at my email today. Sorry. You'll need to bring me up to speed."

"Our email system is getting messed up again. Larry's home computer is the main problem. Because of the things Eddie is doing, Larry's system gets infected with a virus at least once a week."

"I thought you had addressed that issue already. How is it that we can't get this resolved?"

"I need your support David. We have a real problem that I can't solve alone. Eddie is the problem. He keeps violating our company policies and procedures. He's even turning off the virus protection on Larry's system. That's the reason that we keep getting infected again and again."

"Have you talked to Joe or Rick about Eddie?"

"You were at the meeting Tuesday. I thought I had talked to everyone. Eddie just caused the same problem all over again yesterday."

"Eddie's not in my department, shouldn't you be talking to Joe about this? I do support any efforts you make to keep our systems running but some people around here think you're using Eddie as a scapegoat."

"If I can convince you to work with me I will either prove what I'm saying is true or I'll prove that Eddie isn't the problem? If I can get you and everyone in management to help me stop Eddie from doing anything to any of our computer systems for two weeks I guarantee that we will not have an email issue of any kind. If we still have any issue with our email system, then Eddie is not the problem. What do you think David?"

"I don't know anything about IT issues but I do believe in your skills and your integrity. If you say Eddie's causing a problem, then we need to get it stopped."

"I've asked for a management meeting at 9:30 this morning. I'll be counting on your support."

"That wasn't on my schedule and I really don't have…"

Craig interrupted, "I need you to be there. Can I count on you?"

"I'll be there. What you've said to me today has made a lot of sense, but you need to relax. You'll communicate a lot better if you let some of that anger go."

"This whole thing has been so frustrating. I've already tried to work this out with Joe and I'm just not getting the support I need to do my job. I know what I'm doing around here. You know me, David, I'm doing the best I can. Thanks for listening."

As Craig left my office, I hoped he had heard my advice because he really needed to relax. He was about to explode. Just as I started to look at my email, my phone rang. It was Rick.

"I need you to come to my office right now."

"I was trying to check on the outsourcing…"

"David, come to my office now."

I hung up the phone and headed towards Rick's office as quickly as I could. Rick's voice was cold and distant; he didn't sound like himself at all. You could feel the tension in the room. Joe, Larry, Jim and Rick were all seated around the conference table. Larry and Jim looked like two guys that just wanted to stay out of the way. Joe was bouncing with nervous energy and looked like he was ready for combat. He could hardly sit still in his chair as he fumbled with one of the remote controls. Rick looked up and said, "Thanks for coming so quickly. Shut the door."

"We ought to find a way to bottle the energy in this room." My attempt at humor wasn't received well at all so I quickly continued with "You didn't tell me everyone was coming. Where's Craig?"

"Craig wasn't invited." It was all too obvious that Rick was in no mood for humor. He continued with his agenda as he said, "As you all are aware, we are currently having some financial difficulties. Those conditions are forcing us to make some changes around here. Part of those changes will be a reduction in the number of staff members we have. None of us like this but it is the reality that we're faced with. We've got to do something and I need everyone's input."

No one said a word and as I looked around the room it looked like everyone was trying to become invisible. Everyone was looking at their laptops, their shoes, the floor; we were all just trying to avoid anything to do with this conversation or the issues at hand. Before I knew it, I had opened my big mouth and said, "What are we talking about Rick?"

As Rick began to speak he looked off into space. It was almost as if he was trying to separate himself from what he was doing. His body language was saying that he didn't want to be associated with the words coming out of his mouth. He avoided eye contact and spoke in a monotone voice. "Everyone in this room knows we've got a problem with our IT department. Craig just isn't getting the job done. Craig blew up at a meeting yesterday afternoon and then again in my office. He has had the nerve to ask for us all to change our schedule today so he can offer us another excuse as to why we can't get off this "blacklist" thing. I think we're all tired of not being able to use our email. Craig and his staff have a lot of excuses but not many answers. We all know that we have to cut back on staff somewhere. Why don't we cut back and eliminate a problem at the same time. Do you, as my management team, think we need to get rid of Craig and find someone else to run that department?"

Joe exploded to his feet with the enthusiasm of a racehorse seeing the finish line after a long, hard race. "Let me start off by saying that I have tried to support and work with Craig. It hasn't worked. He is so insecure about his lack of knowledge that he attacks people like Eddie who are trying to help him. Craig thinks that no one around here knows enough about IT to realize that he and his staff just aren't getting the job done. Eddie has a good understanding of what type of services we need from our IT department. Eddie could run the IT department and we could still have his input on engineering issues. It's a move that solves our IT problem, saves money and let's us keep someone that brings an awful lot to this company. I vote that we let Eddie get the job done in our IT department and that we let Craig go."

I asked, "When did you lose confidence in Craig?"

"How can anyone be expected to have confidence in a person who gives us a system that doesn't work? Craig and his staff just haven't gotten the job done. Luckily, I've had someone in my own department to help me with IT issues. Eddie has been helping me send emails to Germany for over a month now."

"Didn't Craig say we could have sent emails to Germany all along if we used helpdesk?"

"Yeah David, helpdesk really works, and the tooth fairy is real!! Things in helpdesk never get done, they just get lost in there. That's why I don't put requests into helpdesk. Craig says that helpdesk is the only thing he'll deal with because it's documented. It's a documented failure if you ask me. Its simple David, if I need something fixed on my computer, I should be able to call or ask someone from that department to fix it. This is just common sense. We don't have to complicate the issue here."

As Joe spoke I remembered what my wife had said when we had talked about what was going on at work. She said, "We have two children, a mortgage, 3 cars and college expenses to think about. You're making more money at your job than you're going to make anywhere else in this town. Keep your mouth shut and ride this out. Rick will snap out of his trauma soon and business will pick. This isn't a time for standing up for principles, it's a time for keeping your job and paying your bills."

I didn't respond to Joe as I took my wife's advice and shut my mouth. I did offer one of those politically correct smiles that were supposed to give Joe the reassurance that he needed. He could feel assured that he had made his point. I didn't feel good about this but I did it.

Jim said, "You guys need to understand that if we don't raise some cash, cut back on payroll and get rid of some of this inventory we aren't going to be around for long. We've got more staff than we need and way too much inventory. We've ramped up in anticipation of what we thought would be 60 million dollars in sales. Gentlemen, we will be lucky to do 5 million in sales for the year. Something has got to give here."

Larry spoke up, "We've got the luxury of parents with very deep pockets Jim. We'll be around for a long time. You don't need to worry. You're part of the management team and you need to show everyone your faith in what we're doing. We're going to be OK."

"Don't fool yourself Larry. Our parent companies aren't going to just throw more money our way. We've already gone through a lot of their money. They're expecting us to show some business skills before they do anything. If we don't show them that we know how to handle these issues, they will handle them for us. After they're done with cleaning up our mess, they'll get rid of us. Then they'll find someone that can take care of business and run this company. We have to raise cash, cut back on staff and get rid of some of this inventory."

"Let's get back on track guys. We are cutting back on staff, that's not the issue. The issues are do we let Craig go and do we let Eddie run our IT department?"

Jim looked troubled as he asked, "I know Eddie is a good engineer but how am I supposed to know enough about his IT skills to even have an idea as to whether or not he can run our IT department? Running an IT department involves more than just sending emails. Everything we do involves using the computer systems."

Joe was eager to respond with, "I'm telling you this guy is a "Wiz" at computers. He helps all kinds of people around here on computers. He's done everything I've asked him to do. Larry can tell you, Eddie gets it done right and on time. Tell him Larry."

"He's right. Eddie knows what he's doing on computer systems. He got my home system working and has worked on most of the computers in my department. We've been letting him do all kinds of stuff simply because we couldn't get Craig and his staff to do it. I think Eddie will be great." You could see the relief on Larry's face, as I'm sure he had been concerned that this meeting was going to be about cutting some of his sales staff. As a matter of fact you could see that look of relief going around the room as folks jumped on the Eddie bandwagon.

I thought to myself, isn't Larry's system the one that Craig had just finished telling me had caused the email problems to begin with? Didn't he tell me Eddie was the problem? Why were we about to hand over the leadership of our IT department to someone with no real training in IT?

Is this about cost, politics, power and lack of leadership, or am I just having a nightmare? I had told Craig that I would support him and I hadn't. Not a word. I didn't even insist that he be allowed to be present to defend himself. I wasn't supporting the best interest of our company. I was looking out for number 1, myself. I wasn't part of a team. I was part of a lynch mob. We had found a scapegoat. I, like everybody else in the room was just happy it wasn't me.

Jim quickly realized that if he didn't join the mob mentality and help us hang Craig that he might become the mob's next victim. "If you guys support Eddie, so will I. We need to talk about when and how we're going to do this."

"It's going to be done today, at the 9:30 meeting Craig asked for in his email. David, you and I will be the only ones attending Craig's meeting today. I know everyone here was asked to attend but I'm telling you not to be there. David and I will take care of this. We're going to let Craig go."

"What about Craig's staff? You know Craig does have their loyalty. Those guys all have IT experience and credentials. Are they going to be willing to work for Eddie? Does Eddie have any IT training?"

"In this economy we don't have to worry about anyone quitting their job. That's not going to be a problem, David. It's not like these are highly skilled people you know. If Craig's staff won't work with us, we will be just fine, we can outsource. We would probably save money in the process. I hate to say it but IT people are easily replaced. If we have to we can send Eddie and someone else to one of those IT boot camps. If some of Craig's staff wants to stay with us I suggest that we keep them on until things settle down. Then we can let them go and let Eddie outsource any of our IT needs that he can't take care of."

The message was clear. Our IT department was not considered part of the core of our business at all. They can be replaced. It's more like that department is a support function that irritates us every once in a while. It does offer us a scapegoat from time to time. It seemed to me that this type of old school thinking would keep us dependent on our parent's deep pockets forever. We'd better hope they don't ever act like real parents. They might get tired of waiting for us to grow up, show some maturity and make good decisions. They might even get mad and kick us out of the house. We're not ready to be on our own. We're not even ready to ride without training wheels.

"So we're all in agreement that Craig has to go, correct."

Everyone in the room responded, "Correct."

"Fine, that's done. I do count on everyone's discretion. I certainly don't want this information discussed anywhere. David and I will take care of Eddie and Craig. Everyone but David is excused, as I have no other issues to discuss. Thanks for coming and rest assured things are getting better around here."

I stayed seated as Rick shook everyone's hand as they left the room. The tension was gone and an air of relief and giddiness had taken its place. These guys where actually smiling. It was sad to watch. It was even stranger to be a part of. As the room emptied Rick sat back down, looked at me and said, "It's good to have that issue resolved. I think we'll be much better off with Eddie running our IT department, don't you agree?"

"I hope it's resolved. We're putting an awful lot of faith in Eddie. I really hope we're doing the right thing." I hoped that Rick would reassure me.

Rick acted as if he hadn't heard my comments or that he didn't have any concern as to my obvious needs for reassurance as he stated, "I'll take care of telling Craig that he's got to go. I need you as a witness. Do you have any questions?"

"When do you want him to leave? Do you have a plan on how to do this?"

"We'll take care of Craig as soon as we're done with the 9:30 meeting. I don't want him have the chance to go back to his office or have any access to our systems. Eddie pointed out that we've got to protect ourselves in case Craig does something stupid. You never know how someone will react to something like this. He could leave a bug, a virus or bomb in our systems you know."

I couldn't believe my ears. Why were we all wasting our time sitting in this stupid meeting? Rick had already discussed this whole thing with Eddie. He wasn't having a meeting to get our buy-in. The decision had already been made before this "management" meeting ever occurred. It was obvious that the job had already been offered to Eddie. Too many decisions were being made around here in private little meetings. This entire meeting was for the sole purpose of leaving the perception of teamwork. Something we don't have around here. Who's really running things around here? With disgust in my voice I said, "So you've already talked to Eddie about this change?"

"I had to ask him if he thought he could do this. I talked to him first thing this morning."

I bit my tongue, counted to 10 and tried to remember what my wife had said about why I was still working here. I tried to move on to another subject as I said. "I don't think we need to worry about Craig. I'd like to be able to do this as professionally and courteously as possible."

"Of course we will. You know I'll keep this professional. I was just talking about avoiding problems. Speaking of problems, I will have a security guard waiting to escort Craig out of the building."

"Do you really think that's needed? We've worked with Craig a long time. He's got to be able to go to his office. What about his personal stuff at his desk."

"The guard can get it for him."

I needed this to be over, at least for a few minutes. We weren't only taking Craig's job away from him; we weren't even giving him the respect that he deserved. I'd had enough. "It's your call Rick. I need to go to my office to send out the new presentation so I can find out what our outsourcing options are. You still want me to get that done, don't you?"

"Of course, don't let me hold you up any longer. We will need those services. We still have to cut back on at least four engineers and probably three people in sales."

"OK. I'll see you at 9:30."

As I headed back to my office I wondered if I should be walking upright or slithering like a snake. Somehow I was still walking upright. I reached my desk and sent the presentation to the printer. I dreaded the confrontation that was about to occur with Craig. I wasn't convinced that he deserved what was about to happen. I felt guilty. As I picked up the hard copy of my presentation, I looked up at the clock and realized it was time to go see Craig. I sure hope Craig was feeling more relaxed.

Craig was waiting in the doorway of the conference room when I got there. He didn't seem to be as tense as he had been earlier in the day. He probably thought he was talking to someone he could count on. With that weighing on my conscious I said, "Hey Craig. Are you feeling better?"

"A little. I'll feel a whole lot better when we get these issues resolved."

Rick came into the room and closed the door.

"Rick, Leave the door open. Everyone isn't here yet."

"Everyone that is coming is here. Have a seat Craig."

Looking like someone that has just had the rug pulled out from under him, Craig replied, "I invited the entire management team."

"I know, but it's just going to be us, Craig."

"We need everyone to help solve the issues that I'm dealing with Rick."

"Craig, you've done a wonderful job here and what I'm about to say is in no way a reflection of your job performance."

Craig looked at me for the support that he expected. I couldn't look at anything but my shoes. My stomach was in knots. Craig interrupted Rick and said, "What's going on here? David, answer me. Tell me why you're not talking. You told me you would support me."

"Stop it Craig. This isn't about David. As I was saying what I'm about to say is in no way a reflection of your job performance but more a condition of the market. You've built us a system that's second to none and I personally thank you for your work here. This is a dollars and cents decision Craig. I'm not sure how we're going to get by without you but we have to cut back to survive. Your position has been eliminated."

"You can't eliminate the head of your IT department. You can get rid of me but someone's got to be in charge of your systems. How are you going to run a company with no one in charge of your IT department? You tried that before I was hired and you spent twice as much outsourcing as you have with in house staff. When I came on board your records indicated that your systems were down 40% of the time when you were outsourcing your IT services. Is that what you're going back to? I've done a good job here."

"You've done wonderful things here Craig but with the economic conditions we're facing today we just can't afford to keep the number of staff members we currently have. I think you'll find we've got a nice severance package for you."

"Open your mouth David. Speak. Is this how you support someone?"

"Don't attack David. I told you this isn't about David."

"Just what am I supposed to say Rick?"

Rick was as cold and distant as I've ever seen anyone. He knew what we were doing was wrong and he just couldn't deal with. He wasn't leading our company through rough times. He was shutting down emotionally and using Craig as a scapegoat rather than deal with the real issues at hand. In all the years I've worked with Rick I'd never seen him this much in denial. He just wanted to have this whole thing go away. I realized that I was looking for something in Rick that just isn't there. Maybe it never was. I wasn't any better than Rick. I sat there and didn't do a thing.

We all knew Craig had tried to do his job. He had tried to tell us what was going on with our systems but no one was listening. He had even tried to fix what he thought was wrong but no one would support or help him. Sure he'd made his share of mistakes but not enough to justify this. We were all too busy hoping the focus would just stay on Craig and that no one would start talking about the lack of leadership in our company or the slow sales or the huge adjustments to our books or the missing inventory. Mainly we all hoped that no one would talk about any of our personal and professional failures around here. We had our scapegoat and no one wanted to hear the details. There's plenty of blame to go around, we are all part of this mess.

Rick said, "I would hope that you would understand our position and that we really had no choice. We've worked with each other for a long time. Please don't hesitate to put us down as a reference. We all know you've done a great job here and we'll be glad to say that to anyone. This isn't personal, Craig."

It was obvious that Craig was struggling to keep his emotions under control. "Yes it is. It's very personal to me." He struggled to keep his composure as he continued by asking, "Do you want me to finish out the week?"

"In addition to the severance package you're going to get we will pay you for the rest of the week but I want you to go home right now. There's a security guard waiting to escort you to your car."

"I don't need an escort. That's an insult, Rick. You don't trust me? I deserve better. What about my personal stuff in my office?"

"The guard will get it for you. Let's keep this professional."

"Professional? That's funny Rick. I'll keep this professional all right. I'm just trying to follow the fine examples of professional leadership skills that I've seen around here!"

"We need to move on now. You've got some time to review the package before you accept it. You'll be scheduled to be back here next week to talk with some job placement people if you like."

You could see the shock in Craig's face. This was totally a surprise. He really believed in his work ethics and in what he was saying and doing. It was obvious that in this meeting he had expected to gain the support he needed. We'd hung him out to dry. He was on his own now.

"Yeah, I'm gonna count on you guys for help. You've all been so reliable. Especially you, David."

"Let's go Craig. It's time."

As Rick led him out of the room Craig stopped, turned around, looked right at me and calmly said, "Thanks for your support. Thanks a lot David."

I couldn't even look at him. I did it again. I hadn't said one word. I was disgusted with Rick, my company, what we'd just done but mostly myself.

Craig had just left the doorway when Rick looked back at me, smiled and said, "I think that went well. Don't you?"

I couldn't believe what that idiot just said. I didn't offer a response as I thought, No, I don't think that went well. A human being whom we've worked with for years; that we've trusted and who truly gave us his best efforts just lost his job. I'm not sure he should have lost his job. I am sure that he didn't get the support he had asked for. I need to stop thinking about things I cannot control. I can't right this wrong and I know this was wrong. I need to realize that I still have my job. I need to get busy and change the focus of my day.

As I headed back to my office I saw Eddie rummaging through the things in Craig's old office. That old saying "the body's not even cold yet" came to mind. I was continuing to doubt myself for my participation in the events of the day when I caught a glimpse of Carl (our network administrator), Paul (our database administrator) and Henry (our helpdesk technician) all rushing towards Craig's old office. Let the games begin. The three of them literally picked Eddie up and threw him out of the office. Eddie wasn't very graceful as he flew through the air. It was hard not to laugh out loud as he crashed to the floor and slid up against the wall.

"You just made the mistake of your life. That's my office now and you all work for me."

Carl replied, "If I have to work for you Eddie then I don't work here any more."

Paul and Henry both added, "None of us do."

The three IT nerds were on a mission as they stomped down the hall towards Rick's office. I watched as they went right past a protesting Connie; threw Rick's door wide open with such a force that there was a resounding crash that must have been heard all over the entire plant. Then they all yelled as loud as they could, "We quit. Good luck with your network." The three then turned around and headed right past Eddie, the security guard and out the front door. They looked happy.

As I looked into Rick's office, I could just barely make out his face. The smile was gone from Rick's face. Dazed and confused, he hadn't mustered any response at all to the attack of the IT nerds. I wonder if he even realized his entire IT department had just resigned. As I looked in the other direction I could see Eddie had gotten back up and was back in Craig's old office rummaging through everything. Eddie is a very focused young man. This had been one heck of a morning.

Since the entertainment was over I headed into my office as quickly as I could. I needed to get away so that I might collect my thoughts. I thought about my participation in the events of the day. I couldn't find any value or resolution in my actions. I hadn't been true to myself. As I continued my search for solace, I looked up at the print that I have on my wall.

It has the quote from — Sun Tzu, in The Art of War, *Chapter 3, Verse 18*

"If you know the enemy and know yourself, you need not fear the result of a hundred battles. If you know yourself but not the enemy, for every victory gained you will also suffer a defeat. If you know neither the enemy nor yourself, you will succumb in every battle."

The only warriors I had seen today that had been true to themselves and each other were the nerds. I envied them. I had chosen to stay here with people that did not know the enemy or themselves very well.

I started to get back to work when I noticed a note that I'd left myself to check on the adjustments we'd been making to our books. I'd already talked to Rick about this but his comments hadn't given me much comfort. I wasn't sure where to start so I just printed out a copy of our current balance sheet, inventory control sheets, income statement, etc.. As I looked over the inventory information I noticed that our inventory had an unbelievable amount of adjustments. In the last 8 months alone we had adjusted our inventory 372 times. That's more than 4 adjustments a day. I knew that with those kinds of changes going on for that length of time that there is a strong likelihood that our inventory records are wrong. As I looked further into the matter I found that 4 different people made 98% of these adjustments. I sent out emails to those folks to ask them why they had made so many adjustments to our inventory. I also had some of my staff run a spot check on 5 different inventory items. I was beginning to realize that we didn't have a clue as to what we had in inventory. My thoughts were interrupted by a knock at my door. I said, "Come in."

It was one of my staff, Josh. "I've checked on those inventory items and we're short on every one of them."

I knew that I was about to hear someone verify that our books were wrong. "Just how short are we Jake?"

"They're all off at least 25%. It ranges from 25% to 32%. I've checked twice and we don't have what the records say we have. Do you want me to check some more?"

"No. Thanks for your help. I think I know where the shortages have occurred." I said that just to make Josh feel better about our company. I didn't have a clue where our missing inventory was or why our records weren't accurate. I was so tired of watching this company fall apart. Maybe it wasn't falling apart at all. Maybe we had all been so busy counting the money and growing so fast that we forgot to build a real company. You can't build anything without a foundation and we don't have one. Maybe no one really took a close look until now. I wonder if it's too late.

"I'm glad you're on top of things David. Can I ask you a question?"

"Sure. Go ahead."

"I heard that we're having financial trouble. I heard our books are cooked. Is there any truth to the rumors going around here? Should I be looking for a job?"

I could only hope that I sounded like someone that believed what they were saying when I replied, "We are financially sound. You don't have to worry. Our parent companies are 100% behind us. You don't have to worry about anything, Josh."

"I knew you'd be straight with me. Thanks. Do you need anything else from me?"

"No. Go on back to what you were doing. Thanks for your help."

I leaned back in my chair realizing that if our inventory figures have been wrong then our cost of goods is probably wrong, and our profit and loss has got to be wrong. How in the world is this company in business and why am I here?

I decided that I needed to know more so I called Jim. "Hello Jim. Do you have a couple of minutes that you could give me?"

"Sure David. I'm coming by your office on my way to lunch in about 5 minutes."

"Great. If you could stop in I would appreciate it."

"See you in 5."

True to his word, 5 minutes later Jim was sitting across from me. "How can I help you?"

"Rick and I were discussing the adjustments that have been made to our books and I just needed a clearer understanding."

"No problem. Adjustments are a normal thing in accounting. What adjustments do you want to know about?"

"Let's just pick a number, let's say any adjustment over $50,000.00."

"Most of the adjustments over that amount have involved changes in inventory. I don't know if you're aware of it, but we have had a bit of an inventory problem. Don't worry, I don't mean that we don't have what we need, because we do. Sometimes our records aren't right on the money as far as the amount of inventory we have on hand."

"I'm the VP of Manufacturing. Why wasn't I made aware of these problems?"

"We've had a practice of allowing several different people to make adjustments to inventory. Since you weren't in that group, we didn't see the need to involve you. We've got such a large amount of inventory on hand that it just didn't seem to be an issue for you to be concerned with at this point. You're in charge of manufacturing so we thought your only concern would be having enough inventory on hand to meet your requirements. You have plenty of inventory on hand. By my calculations you've got over 2 ½ years of worth of inventory sitting here."

"I am a business man. As part of our management team, I 'm supposed to offer opinions based on a good working knowledge of the condition of things around here. I would think that knowing the status of our inventory levels and the accuracy of our records would be critical to my ability to offer an educated opinion on anything. How am I supposed to forecast or calculate? How will I know when or what I might need to order? How do we calculate our cost of goods with inventory figures that are wrong?"

"We're close enough."

"What do you mean close enough?"

"You've got to understand that we're not a public company. We don't sell stock. The goal we have here is to satisfy our parent companies expectations. Their perception of our success is all that really matters. I can tell you they are behind us 100%."

"What are they behind? Accounting records that are wrong? What are you talking about Jim? Perception? I'm talking about simple math; you know 2 and 2 equals 4. This company is either doing things right or we aren't. We're either making a profit or we aren't. I can't pay my bills if I don't keep my checkbook balanced. Everything I'm seeing as to our numbers and our record keeping is scaring me to death."

"We need to have this conversation with Rick involved. He can explain this much better than I can. You really don't have to worry. Our company is in great shape. Are you worried about not having enough inventory?"

"I'm beginning to worry about a lot of things around here."

"Let me get with Rick and the three of us can set up a meeting for Friday morning. Until then, don't worry about anything. You know Rick and you know our company is a winner. Any problems we have are problems we can work through together."

"A meeting with the three of us sounds like a good idea. Let me know what time."

"Let's call Connie right now and get it set up."

I dialed Connie's number and said, "Hello Connie. I need to set up a meeting with Rick, Jim and myself for first thing Friday morning."

"I'm sorry David, but Rick is gone until next Tuesday. He and Larry had to make an emergency trip to a customer."

"Thanks Connie. We'll get with him when he gets back."

There was the answer to all my concerns. I don't need to worry about inventory records being wrong, cost of goods being wrong, and profit and loss being off. I don't need to worry because my leader, my boss is running away and playing golf with Larry. He's not worried so why should I be? I should probably get with Jim and go play golf.

"David, are you alright?"

I had truly hoped that this conversation would ease my fears. I wanted to hear that the mistakes I had found were not really mistakes but that they were my errors. I needed to hear that our records were correct. I wanted to hear that our company cared about how and what we did. I didn't want to have my greatest fears confirmed. We as a company are in trouble. It is true that we had parent companies that would probably give us the resources we need to stay in business but they weren't going to give us the business skills and more importantly the integrity to be truly successful. I don't think I can be a part of this for very long. I was startled as I heard Jim speak my name and replied, "What?"

"We'll get together with Rick as soon as he gets back. You don't need to worry."

Why would I worry? I don't need to be concerned that in the last 8 months alone we had adjusted our inventory 372 times. That's more than 4 adjustments a day. I don't need to worry about things like inventory records, cost of goods, profit and loss. I understand when someone is telling me to be quiet, do my job and stop bringing up issues that no one wants to deal with. "I'm fine Jim. I just wanted to help get this straightened out."

With the smile of a South Carolina politician he said, "David I know you and I know you're just trying to help us. You know we will get this straightened out. We are working hard to make things better around here. It's people like you that will make things better."

Make things better... what does that mean? Is that perceptively better or really better? I wanted to tell him to quit blowing smoke but instead I replied, "Thanks for your time Jim. Let me know when we can all get together."

I tried to call my wife but no one was home. I needed to talk to someone I could trust. It was time for lunch so I headed out to my car. I walked past Craig's old office and saw a huge pile of stuff that Eddie had moved out into the hallway. In the pile I could see pictures of Craig's family. As I looked at the pile, I hoped Craig was eventually going to get his personal property back. I remembered that Rick had assured me that the security guard would take care of Craig's personal items. I wondered if Eddie was running the Security department as well as the IT department. Maybe since Rick, Larry, Jim and Craig were all out of the building Eddie's managed to facilitate a bloodless coup. All hail King Eddie! What am I thinking? I regained some measure of control and continued walking out to the parking lot where I ran into Josh.

"David, wait. Let me give you back the projector. I've got it in my car."

I remembered that I had let Jake use one of the company's projectors for his son's birthday party. I was glad that he remembered it as I had completely forgotten about it.

Jake ran to his car and returned with the projector in hand. "Thanks a lot for letting me use it for the kids at my son's party. The video games were awesome. We projected them onto the living room wall. They were huge. There is a problem though. The projector quit working after a couple of hours. I don't think we did anything to it."

"Glad the projector worked for you. Sorry it had a problem. It probably just had a bulb burn out. I'll give it to Craig, I mean Eddie after lunch."

"Eddie? Why would you give it to him?"

"He's running our IT department now. Craig is no longer with us."

"What? When did all of this happen?"

"It all happened today. It's a long story. I'll take care of the projector. I need to get to lunch right now."

"Thanks David. Have a good lunch."

"I will. See you later Josh."

I don't remember getting into my car or the drive to my house. The next thing I do recall is walking in the front door. My wife was there as I walked in the door. She looked at me and said, "What are you doing home? I just got your message."

"I just needed to come home for a bit."

"Are you feeling OK?"

"No. I need to get some rest. I think I'll take the afternoon off."

"Something's wrong. Tell me what it is. I'm here to help."

"Maybe you can help me update my resume." Oh good lord why did I say that out loud. Now she's going to be worried and want some sort of explanation as to what's going on. How can I explain this mess to her when I don't even understand it myself? I should've gone to play golf. Oh no, now I sound like Rick and Larry. Help me please!

ID10T Errors

1. Outsourcing.

Outsourcing projects can offer the potential benefits of access to staff, skill sets and service levels as well as a savings in terms of cost to your organization. Reaching the decision to outsource any portion of an organization's services requires a great deal of needs assessment, business case analysis, transition planning and soul-searching. An outsourcing project has to start with a detailed plan that has a clearly defined beginning, objectives and an ending. At its very best, outsourcing is a risky proposition. Our character David was correct to have concerns about the risk of outsourcing some of the engineering services for his company. David's company seemed to be making the decision to outsource based solely on short term cost benefits. There was no evidence of a long term plan.

In an outsourcing project, contractors and temporary workers are typically given privileged access to your systems and your intellectual property, with little control over or oversight of their activities. That lack of control only increases the potential for theft, fraud, corporate espionage and even cyberterrorism. Outsourcing is just another log on the security fire that's burning our company down. David should be afraid, very afraid.

The outsourcing vendor that you choose is given a unique opportunity to understand your business in depth. The vendor needs to build relationships with your business peers and learn as much as possible about you and your business in order to fulfill your requirements and do a good job. During this process the vendor actually begins to build a knowledge base about you and your business. That knowledge base will make it harder for you to change your outsourcing choice once the contract is up. It will also give the vendor an unfair advantage in future sourcing opportunities. You need to always maintain a competitive environment when dealing with outsourcing vendors.

Methods to create competitive events in your sourcing arrangement:

· Competitively bid some services to keep pricing and terms realistic.

· Give other vendors the opportunity to learn about your needs and build their own knowledge base as to your company.

· Do whatever is needed to prevent any one vendor from having a lock on your business.

The creation of the right type of relationships with your vendor and your business partners are one of the key elements of any outsourcing success. The vendor must clearly understand what you will consider as acceptable interactions with your business partners. If you do not properly manage and lead all aspects of your project, your function could be perceived as little more than the management of the project. At that point the vendor will become a surrogate or, worse, a rival.

You can minimize these types of risks and maintain identities by:

- Maintaining close ties with business partners.
- Asserting your leadership.
- Recruiting your peers to help keep your team in charge.
- Making and/or participating in all training and technology decisions.
- Clearly defining expectations, acceptable vendor actions and interactions.

Outsourcing, like most projects, normally start out with high expectations, excitement, tension, lots of involvement and a detailed plan. Some of the risks involved will normally come to light about midstream in an outsourcing project as the different needs and constraints of the parties involved become apparent. At that point in a project, it is normal for the parties involved to grow increasingly suspicious and self-protective. The strain of tight budgets, time lines and constant communications will further test everyone's skills and determination. Outsourcing projects that incorporate the minimal steps listed below will hopefully avoid ending up in the tank.

Successful outsourcing projects include:

- A clearly defined plan of action.
- Speaking a common language.
- Negotiating effectively.
- Openness to new ideas.
- Strong management with a life cycle approach.
- Maintaining the training of internal staff to the skill levels they need to make good decisions and if needed manage the outsourcing arrangements.
- Openness to new processes and procedures.
- Making technology decisions and participating in all training.
- Not forgetting the human issues that are involved.
- Constantly measuring the results.
- An exit strategy.

2. Foundations, Trust, Integrity and Value.

"I don't think I can be a part of this for very long." That's where David our VP of Manufacturing is; he is a victim. David, a top employee who has worked at our company for many years is considering resignation. He has access to important files, system information, intellectual property and he knows our history. He is ready to take his skills, his experiences, his contacts and himself out of this organization. As a senior member of our management team and our VP of Manufacturing he knows our company, our products, our staff strengths, our testing methods, our marketing skills and our weaknesses. Our fictional company doesn't seem to be concerned or even aware of the great potential danger that losing a long time employee like David represents. Staff members who are considering resignation may be removing information without any malicious intent or wish to harm or cause havoc. They may be copying files, such as customer lists, trade secrets, client records and other intellectual properties from projects to document their work history and build their portfolios. These are some of the risks our company is being exposed to if David is ethical. If he isn't ethical, the level of risk our company is being exposed to includes things like theft, fraud and corporate espionage.

Our company is also running the risk that a competitor could soon be hiring David. A competitor would love to have someone on their staff that knows what our assets are, what our products are, how they've been designed, tested, manufactured and how best to compete with them. All of the investments our company has made in David over all those years of working together could potentially be used against our company should David end up working for a competitor.

Perception, close enough, 372 inventory adjustments in 8 months! Somehow these things just weren't inspiring the sense of purpose, the trust, loyalty and the confidence David was searching for. Companies whose employees understand and share the mission and goals of the organization enjoy higher productivity and growth. People want their work to make a difference. Mission statements and core values statements are methods that companies use to express organizations intentions. They should be an honest reflection of the values and principles that matter to the organization. They should refine the organization's aspirations and guide its actions! Our company needs some guides.

The staff in our company no longer trusts each other. The lack of leadership and integrity has eroded whatever trust there was. David does not feel like a valued staff member. He no longer values his involvement with this company. He is a reflection of a system that has no foundation and that has caused its own security issues.

Mission statements and core value statements can't help this or any company if they are just words on a piece of paper. They could be used as a tool to refine the organizations aspirations, guide its actions and motivate its staff if they were actually implemented! This company does need some motivation.

Some examples of mission statements and core values:

- ACCOUNTABILITY - Take responsibility for decisions at the individual & company levels.
- ATTITUDE – We can, we will, we do.
- BALANCE – Family, fun and work.
- CHALLENGE - We strive to be more than we were yesterday.
- COMMITMENT – Our word is our bond.
- QUALITY – We strive to exceed the expectations of customers and ourselves everyday and in everything we do.

- VALUE – We value what we do, who we are, our customers, their expectations, our guest, our partners, our families, our expectations and our fellow employees.

Some of the elements that comprise a good foundation are:

- Trust based on integrity between management and employees.
- Creation of a value system that places true value on everyone and everything involved.
- Clearly define and share the mission, goals and standards.
- Constantly measure and redefine all of these efforts.

3. Theft.

Josh used the company projector for his child's party. Josh had gotten permission from David. David knew that Josh was going to use it for personal use. The bulb burned out during Josh's child's birthday party. That's a small matter, but it is theft. The company is experiencing a $500.00 expense to replace the burned out bulb. If this use was some type of a reward for some good job performance or a standard use of the equipment it might not be considered theft. With the limited information we are given in this story it does represent an expense that at the very least the company could ask Josh to pay for. I doubt Josh would have agreed to use the projector if he thought it could cost him $500.00. If this practice of usage is widespread that expense could grow exponentially and become a real security issue. There should be written policies and procedures for proper equipment usage. The enforcement of a written policy would eliminate any issues associated with this matter.

4. The threat from within.

Security threats are always evolving. You can never rest easy for long. It's crucial to look beyond the obvious external security threats and to prepare for the threat from within. Think about it. Who knows better how to penetrate, damage or simply wreak havoc on your systems and your company—a competitor, a hacker or an employee down the hall? Internal attacks and misuse of properties present a much greater risk than external attackers. The motivation for employees to cause serious damage to your systems, your information and ultimately your company range from greed, ambition, stress, power struggles, to long-standing grudges. One of the most frequently overlooked dangers to your organization probably doesn't have to have anything to do with "blacklist", bugs, worms, viruses, weak firewalls, or technology at all—its probably someone you know by name—in our company that danger is Eddie. It is said that, in the absence of true leadership, demons will rush in to fill the void. In our story, it does seem that Eddie has a couple of horns growing out of his head. He is a demon of sorts and he definitely has a plan to fill the void. Eddie has a malicious intent and a desire to harm or cause havoc in an attempt to further his own career. As part of his plan for takeover, Eddie does use technology as a tool to wreak havoc with the email system. Don't be distracted with the technology though; Eddie is the real threat.

The quality of your products and the issues you have to deal with are a direct reflection of the environment you have created to work in. Investments in your environment such as clearly defining goals and standards, trusting and valuing each other and sharing are some of the very best methods of protecting yourself from the risks associated with security issues.

Eddie thrives in an environment where the tactics of manipulation are stronger than those of good business, where the perception of a dedicated worker is stronger than the reality of a dedicated employee. The lack of real business skills, poor business foundations, no leadership, the stress of slow business and continuous power struggles have all worked in Eddie's favor. Eddie is a master manipulator. How else could one explain that an engineer, who doesn't finish his assigned projects, violates company policies and surfs adult web sites at work ends up being promoted and running the IT department?

Somewhere between 50% and 80 % of the value of any business is in its intellectual property. In most businesses today, 95% of that intellectual property is stored on computer systems. There are inherent risks that come with putting corporate information on computer systems, just as there are inherent risks in most forms of human communication and endeavors. The real security issues of today cross all kinds of boundaries. They not only concern attacks on your technical systems, but your company's management, your communications and your business structure are all subject to attacks. Attackers like Eddie will almost always take the easiest and most convenient route to exploit and wreak havoc within your organization. While their motives may vary, people like Eddie are in constant search of any vulnerability. They count on the organization's inability to fix problems. To truly have any real security, you must constantly monitor your environment, your systems, your efforts and you always need to know who and what you're dealing with. We all have to live up to the challenge of proactively seeking, identifying, and eliminating internal and external security threats and vulnerabilities. Your success and your company's success depend on it.

Typical reasons external enemies attack:

- Joy riders normally just trying to show off their skills; some are more malicious.
- Politics/Political messages
- Theft, fraud, corporate espionage and even cyberterrorism.

Typical reasons internal enemies attack:

- To exploit and wreak havoc within your organization.
- It's easy and convenient to attack from within; insiders know what your assets are, where they're stored and how to access them.
- Theft, fraud, corporate espionage and even cyberterrorism.
- Ambition, greed, malicious intent or wish to harm or cause havoc.

Know your friends, your enemies and yourself. That knowledge offers you one of the best methods to defend against internal and external threats. You need to have a full and complete understanding of your systems, your staff, your company and the security risks associated with all of them. Know your points of vulnerability. You need to take the steps needed to protect yourself.

5. Visibility and Leadership.

The responsibility for the environment in any organization lies directly at the feet of the leadership within that organization. Bad things happen when there is an environment that allows them to continue to occur. In this portion of story our CEO, Rick, eliminated an employee (Craig) who had attempted to address issues that the company needed to resolve. Rick set several bad examples during and after these events. Rick doesn't deal with issues very well. He expects to be given an immediate solution from his staff. From his perspective that's why he hired them. He refuses to be involved with the details of an issue. Rick doesn't feel a responsibility to understand or actively participate in such matters. If a staff member attempts to force Rick's involvement they do so at their own peril as is evidenced with Craig's elimination. Rick's treatment of Craig and his staff seriously eroded any foundations that existed within our company. The damage from such actions could be widespread and long term.

Management further exhibited its destructive nature as it allowed business decisions to be made in small private meetings. There wouldn't be a problem with that action if it were the normal and stated methods of operation within this business. The problem surfaced when members of the "management team" realized that their input was no longer relevant. Those private meetings were held in advance of the "management team" meeting. The "management team" meeting served no purpose other than to offer the perception of teamwork to staff members who were not privy to the real situation. It was nothing but an attempt to deceive. The decisions to remove Craig and to allow Eddie to run the IT department had already been made. These types of actions cause irreparable harm to the trust and to the value systems that are needed within a company in order for it to be successful.

When a major event occurs such as the elimination of staff member(s), change of responsibilities, or anything that could potentially change the work environment the leadership of a company needs to maintain a high level of visibility. That visibility will give the remaining staff the security and a sense of stability that is needed to recover from the trauma… Rick must have put his Wizard hat on just after the IT nerds resigned because that visionary did one heck of a vanishing act, didn't he? He left the building! He went to play golf! In our story Connie gave David some lame excuse that Rick and Larry had supposedly gone to see a client. I refer to it as lame excuse because Rick's responsibility at that moment was to his company and his staff. They needed his presence! He wasn't there! He hasn't been there for a long time.

Friday

My name is Jane and I'm the resident eye candy around here. At least I'm smart enough to know that some of the idiots that I'm forced to work with have that perception of me. Their maturity level peeked somewhere around the 10th grade. They got stuck there and never progressed any farther. Don't get me wrong, I know that I am an attractive young woman and I know that I look good in a short, tight skirt, a low cut blouse and three-inch heels. Sometimes I'll even use that approach if I think it will work or is needed. I'm someone with a lot of skills, intelligence and desire. I have a Master's in marketing from Pepperdine University. Working two jobs and carrying a full academic load, I put myself through school in 7 years.

I can remember being thrilled at the opportunity to become a part of this company. That was almost two years ago, back when this company was the hottest ticket around. At that time it appeared to be on the edge of greatness. My first year here was nothing short of great. It was fun. Everybody exceeded their goals, sales were out the roof, anything you asked for you got and everything was first class. I really thought I would be here for a long time. The world looked beautiful through those rose colored glasses we all wore. None of us saw what was coming. When our sales started to slow down, they didn't just slow down; they fell off the charts. We weren't prepared. We didn't know what to do. As sales have continued to slip away, we all have begun to grow increasingly suspicious and self-protective. We certainly aren't pulling together as a team. We're tearing this place apart. Unfortunately I think I've already seen this company at its peak.

When our sales dropped, it was the first time that I really had an opportunity to take a good look at this company and the people I was working with. I soon realized that our baby was ugly. We were all used to working in an environment with little control or oversight of our efforts and activities. We never really had worked as a team.

It's gotten so bad around here that I question whether or not this company will survive. This company will have to make drastic changes if it's going to survive. We need leadership, structure and a plan. I don't have much faith in the idiots we have running this place. Those are the same guys that created an environment where everyone did whatever they wanted. As my dear old Daddy used to say, "Too many Generals and not enough soldiers and you'll lose the battle." This company is going nowhere fast. I'm just treading water and making sure I get good references from these clowns. I've already got my resume out. My future isn't going to be sinking with this ship of fools. It is entertaining however to watch the circus of events and power struggles that are constantly going on around here. I'm not sure why anyone would want to stay here. Why would anyone want to stay in the asylum when it looks like the patients have already taken over? This job is simply a paycheck until I get my career back on track somewhere else.

It's Friday morning and I've watched this place go absolutely crazy all week long. I'm ready for the weekend. This week has been particularly stressful as our sales levels continue to drop. I honestly don't see us turning things around. There is no evidence of a plan or the leadership to even formulate a plan of action. As a matter of fact our great leader is not even in the building today. He has gone to find his answers at the golf course as usual. Larry's business plan is to stay calm, play golf and wait for the business to return. That's all he's got. He really expects everyone to buy into that. Scary. Larry doesn't know what to say or what to do. He's not a leader. He's an order taker. His idea of a marketing plan is to take the client out, get them drunk, play golf and take them to a dance club. That's it, that's all he has to give. I used to think that Rick, our CEO, would recognize Larry's inability to lead this department and make some changes. Unfortunately the more I've gotten to know Rick the less hope I have for this company. Our CEO likes to pat people on the back and tell about his visions but he doesn't have a clue how to run a business. That is the type of talent we have around here. These guys are running the place. Things like this used to really bother me, but I'm learning to let it go. It helps that I've decided I'm just along for the ride and I don't need to worry about this company's future anymore. I can do my job, keep my mouth shut and charm my way right past these idiots. It won't be long before I am out of this mess.

The document on my computer screen was completely locked up. I hate it when that happens. I was trying to finish a presentation that I was making for a client and I needed to get it out to them today. I really dreaded what I had to do now. The whole process you have to go through is ridiculous. I knew that if I called down to IT they would tell me to put a request into helpdesk. That statement is so irritating since we all know that I can't send a message to helpdesk if my computer is locked up. Then I'll get to have a conversation about how am I supposed to send a request to helpdesk if my computer doesn't work. I wonder if they just do this to jerk us around. I should be able to call them to come fix my computer. I wish those guys would practice some better customer service skills.

Knowing that I didn't have a choice, I called the IT extension. When they answered the phone I didn't give them a chance to speak. I said, "My computer is locked up. I know you want me to run this through your helpdesk but I can't send you a helpdesk request with my computer because it's not working. If you fix it for me, I'll send you a helpdesk thank you note. Can somebody help me? Please help me. I've got to get this presentation finished and sent out to my client today."

"Is that you Jane?"

At least that was a different response. I replied, "Yes, who is this?"

"It's Eddie. Don't you recognize my voice?"

"I'm sorry, I meant to call helpdesk but maybe you can help me. My computer is locked up and I need to get some work done."

"I can be there in about 5 minutes. While I've got you on the phone let's try something. Reboot your computer. Do you know how to do that?"

"I can do that but will I lose everything I've worked on this morning?"

"You will lose any changes you've made since the last time you saved your work. You do save your work frequently, don't you?"

"You know, I think I did save it just before it locked up."

"Great. Let's reboot your system. I'll hold on while you reboot. By the way, you did dial the helpdesk. I guess you haven't heard that I'm in charge of the IT department now."

"Really... Congratulations. What happened to Craig?" As I congratulated Eddie I did wonder why we were putting an engineer in charge of our IT department. I thought we were supposed to be a high tech sort of company?

"Craig had been having a lot of problems working with a lot of people around here for quite a while. The IT department just wasn't functioning as it should and things just weren't getting done. He blew up a couple of times the other day and Rick had just had enough. Craig's no longer a member of our family."

I thought "family"; we're not a family. What's he talking about? Maybe he meant some weird dysfunctional family. Just then my computer came back up and prompted me for my password. "Its back up and running now. I guess that took care of it."

"Great! It was probably just an ID10T Error. That should take care of it. Call me back if you need anything else."

"I will. Thanks Eddie and congratulations again on your new job."

As I typed in my password I wondered if the rest of our IT staff was still here. I sure hope they are. I know they had a tremendous loyalty to Craig, but we need them. Eddie knows a little bit about IT, but I don't think he has enough knowledge to run our systems. My computer wasn't accepting my password; it prompted me for my password again. After a couple more attempts I called helpdesk back.

"This is Eddie. How can I help you?"

"It's me, Jane. This thing isn't accepting my password. I can't get logged on at all."

"Check to make sure you're using the proper case for your password as passwords are case sensitive."

"I know that, Eddie. It's not working. Could you please come and help me?"

"Sure, I'll come help you. Don't get frustrated. Give me about 5 minutes. I'm sorry we couldn't fix it over the phone and I understand you've got work you need to get done. I'll have it running for you in no time."

"Thanks." As I hung up, I was pleased with the responsiveness Eddie was giving me. It looked like I would be back up and working in no time. That's the kind of customer service an IT department should be giving us. Maybe Eddie's going to make a difference around here.

True to his word, 5 minutes later Eddie came walking into my office. He was smiling that Cheshire cat type of smile. He was so full of himself. Obviously he thought he was Mr. Big shot now. "Let me help get you back to work." As he sat behind my computer he smiled and asked, "How have you been?"

"Great. I'll be even better if you can help me get this thing working. I need to get some things done. I'd love to get out of here about 4:30 today."

He continued working on my computer as he said, "Big plans for the weekend?'

"Not that big. I've got some friends from college coming for a visit and I'd like to get home to freshen up before they get there."

"You always look great, girl. You don't need to freshen up."

I could tell from the look on his face that whatever Eddie was trying to do on my computer wasn't working the way he wanted it to. I asked, "Isn't it letting you logon either?"

"It will. It's just being finicky. Don't worry I'll have you back up in just a minute. Are these guests of yours old girlfriends?"

"Yes. One of them was an old roommate and the other was one of the girls we always ran around with."

"Are they single?"

"Yes they both are, but I think they have boyfriends. Are you trying to get me to fix you up, Eddie?" I really hoped he would just get my computer fixed and this conversation would end. My girlfriends wouldn't be the least bit interested in Eddie.

"If they look like you I'd love to meet them. I don't really go out very much you know."

Eddie was talking about my friends but his body language was telling me his real focus was with the problem on my computer that he was working on. It looked as if that problem on the computer was about to get the best of him. He was sweating, squirming and looked concerned.

I was trying to think of a way to avoid hurting his feelings but at the same time letting him know that my friends were off limits when he said, "I'm going to have to go reset your password on the server. What would you like to change it to?"

"Let's try TGIF1"

"It's got to be at least 7 letters and 1 number."

"Let's go with Its1Friday"

"That'll work. Write it down some place just in case you forget it. It will take me about 15 minutes to get everything changed. I'll call you when you can log back in. Sorry for the delay. I guess your records got contaminated or something."

"Don't worry I'll remember the password. Thanks for your help. I've got some phone calls I can make while I wait for my computer. If my line is busy call back or leave a message."

Eddie left the room and I felt assured that he would have my computer up and running again soon. The phone calls were something that I needed to do today anyway, so I wasn't wasting time. I still had a chance of getting out of the office early.

Just as I started to dial the phone, Jerry stuck his head in my office doorway and said, "Are you having trouble logging into the network?"

I didn't have time for Jerry today. He's a professional at appearing to be busy while never actually doing a thing. I replied, "Yes I am. I've got Eddie working on it. Are you having trouble too?"

"Yeah, but I'm sure Eddie will get it fixed. What do you think about all of the changes around here lately?"

"You mean Eddie being in charge of running the IT department?"

"Eddie is the only person left in our IT department. All of those nerds in IT had an attack of loyalty or stupidity; I'm not sure which it was. They all quit their jobs yesterday. Eddie is running the show all by himself."

It's hard to focus on anything Jerry ever says because he is such a pig. Every time he speaks to me his eyes are focused on my boobs the entire time. It's like he's waiting for me to jump up on the desk, take off my top and give him a show like some of those girls in the dance clubs he goes to. It's very hard to take this frat boy seriously. He's offensive; he knows it and he doesn't care. He doesn't come in here to talk to me. He comes in here to look at me. I did hear that he just said Eddie was all-alone in our IT department. That concerned me a little. We were certainly putting a lot of faith in Eddie all of the sudden. Hope it works.

"Are you sure that they all quit? What could possibly have made all of those guys in IT quit?"

"I heard that Eddie had to throw the nerds out of Craig's office and that they all got mad, burst into Rick's office like a bunch of idiots and just quit. Those guys probably knew Eddie wouldn't put up with them not getting things done around here."

"I'm not sure that having just one person in a department is good for us. Can Eddie do all of the work that those guys were doing? What if he gets sick or hurt?"

"You don't need to worry about Eddie. He'll keep our systems running. He knows what he's doing and is very good at what he does. He won't let us down. I'm sure he's got some backup planned if he gets sick or hurt."

As Jerry spoke, I thought about the makeup of our Sales department. Larry the idiot is in charge. That's really all you need to say about Larry's skills. He treats Jerry like his fair-haired wonder boy. Everything Jerry has here or has done here has been handed to him on a silver platter. Jerry just doesn't have what it takes when it comes to being a salesman. He's like most spoiled brats I've ever seen. He expects everything to be handed to him. Jerry would cut his mentors throat in a heartbeat for a chance to get ahead.

Then you have me. I'm obviously intelligent, skilled, attractive, frustrated, jealous, suffering under an environment full of sexual harassment, under utilized and definitely not appreciated. I couldn't continue with this pointless mental review of our Sales staff, as it was just too depressing.

Those IT nerds had the strength and integrity to stand up for what they believed in. I couldn't think of any other department in this company where there was any loyalty at all. I admired the degree of commitment those guys had shown. They seemed to believe in what they were doing, each other and they sure made the ultimate sacrifice. They gave up their jobs to make a point. I wouldn't be able to do that. I did admire what they did but I'm not sure it was smart. What about job references? You don't leave a job until you have another job. Oh well, I'm a career minded person. We all have our priorities.

"Have you seen David around? I need to get some samples for a client from inventory. He said something to me the other day about a new procedure we needed to use to get samples. Do you know how we're supposed to get samples? I need to get these sent out today."

"I tried to find him first thing this morning. He's not going to be here today. He had mentioned something to me about that inventory thing too. I tried to tell him that we're trying to document way too much around here. I don't want to have to fill out a tax return worth of paperwork to get samples for my clients. It's ridiculous. After he told me that we were going to have to use this new request form and some other paper work,

I just went straight back there and loaded up on plenty of samples of everything. I've got enough samples for the next two years. Hopefully by the time I run out of samples David will have figured out that we don't need to make getting samples for our clients so complicated. David is really disappointing me. He knows me and he knows I don't want to steal any inventory. We're making everything around here too complicated. Come to my office this afternoon and I'll take care of you. You can have whatever you need. Don't mention anything about this to anyone."

"Thanks for helping me get some samples. Don't worry, I won't tell anyone. What's going on around here? Is there anyone from management left in the building? What do you think about Larry and Rick taking off again? This place is going crazy. I'll stop by and get what I need later."

"They didn't just take off. They're taking care of a client. Hopefully they'll get some orders. I hope they can get some time alone to come up with some ideas to get our sales turned around."

"They're playing golf Jerry! I doubt they'll solve anything more than Rick's slice. You and I have both been out with Larry and Rick on these type of events. They don't solve business issues out there. They try to forget about business and just pretend everything is OK."

Just then my phone rang. It was Eddie. I could tell we had big problems just from the tone of his voice. He didn't sound full of himself anymore. He sounded scared. He told me that he'd run into some problems and that it would be a while before I could get back onto the system. He said something about server issues or a firewall configuration I really didn't pay much attention to the details. Once I understood that my computer wasn't going to be working I had all of the information I needed. As soon as I got off the phone I looked back at Jerry and said, "It looks like Eddie is having some big problems in IT. We won't be using our computers this morning."

"What do you mean?"

"That was Eddie and he says it's going to be a while before he can get things working again."

"What did he say was wrong?"

"I don't know, I think he said something about server issues or a firewall configuration, I don't really know. Call him if you want the details. All I do know is that I've got to figure something out because I've got company coming and I need to get out of here early today."

"I'll go see Eddie and see if I can help. See you later."

I really didn't want to think that Jerry was going to be working on our computer systems. At least he left my office. Sometimes to get him out of your office, you have to remove him with a bulldozer or a crane. When he's not traveling and playing golf, Jerry just sort of wanders around the building trying to look busy. If he spent as much time being busy as he spends trying to look busy, he'd get a lot done. It's a shame that Jerry doesn't have some direction or purpose. He hasn't found any of those qualities in himself and it doesn't appear that he knows how to even begin to look for them. As he left my office, I couldn't help but think about what those nerds in IT had done. Maybe those nerds could have shown Jerry some of the qualities he needs. Who am I kidding? Those guys weren't cool enough for Jerry to listen to.

I needed a boost so I headed towards the break room to get some coffee. As I entered the room I saw Jim pouring himself a cup of our best Java. Jim seems to be enjoying what he does around here. It is refreshing to see that someone around here is enjoying something. I looked at him with a big smile and said, "Hi Jim. How's your day going?"

"It's always good to see you Jane. As for my day, I've had better. Something has gone wrong on my computer and I can't get logged on to the network. Those machines are great when they work but when they don't, they keep me from getting anything done. Sometimes I wish we didn't rely on them so much."

"It's not just your computer Jim. Jerry and I can't get anything done either. Have you talked to Eddie yet? You do know that he's in charge if IT now, don't you?"

"I've already left him a message. Yes I did I hear about the changes in IT. I guess we've put Eddie to the test right off the bat. He sure didn't have to wait long to have some IT issues to fix did he?"

"Eddie told me it would be a while before I could use my system. I guess he's run into some issues. I'm sure he'll take care of things. He has helped me with a lot of computer stuff in the past. What do you think about Craig's staff quitting the way they did?"

"Craig's staff has always been very loyal to him. Craig was very good at putting talented folks together and building a team. I'm afraid he wasn't very good at realizing that the team was our entire company and not just his department. His poor communication skills caused those guys to feel isolated and defensive. Maybe they should have been more loyal to the company. I don't think they helped their careers with that kind of move. I'm sure they saw it as a loyalty thing. The fact is they're gone and they didn't have to be."

"I've never heard of an entire department quitting. It's weird. I don't know if I admire them or feel sorry for them. Oh well, I've got to get back to my office. Have a good weekend."

"Before you go I'd like to get your input on something. How do you think your clients would react if we were to run a 25% off sale on products purchased within the next 90 days? Do you think we could generate some sales?"

"To tell you the truth, I don't really think that would cause my clients to buy any more of our products right now. It would take a much larger discount than that to even get their attention and I'm not sure that would even work. You've got to understand most of my clients already have a surplus of our products in their inventory. That's why the market is so dead. Frankly, if it wasn't for the purchases being made by our parent companies, I don't know what we would do for sales around here."

"I'm just searching for ideas, Jane. Let me know any time that you have any ideas on ways to get things moving. We've got a ton of inventory just sitting around here costing us money. Thanks for your time. See you later."

As I headed back to my office, Connie came walking towards me. Connie is the only person in this company that is always in a good mood. She's a joy to be around. I could tell as she walked towards me that something was wrong because she wasn't giving me that big welcome smile. I said, "This must be serious Connie because I've never seen you without that beautiful smile. What's bothering you?"

"I can't get my work done. Rick counts on me getting things done around here and I can't get anything done without my computer. I've got some things that I have to get done this morning. My computer won't let me connect to the network. I can't send an email or anything. I called Eddie and I really don't think he knows when our systems will be back up. How am I supposed to get my work done?"

"If it makes you feel any better everyone I've talked to is having the same problem with their computers. I'm sure Eddie will have us all back on line soon."

"Eddie's not having such a good start at his new position is he? It's gotta be rough on him, this being his first day in charge of IT."

"I'm sure he'll be OK. He will get it fixed for us."

"Any coffee left in there? I could use a cup."

"I'm sure they'll fix you up. Let me know if I can help with anything. I'd like to see you get that smile back. We all count on you and that wonderful smile."

She gave me that smile as she looked back and said, "Thanks Jane. Have a good day."

I was walking towards my office when I realized that our entire network must be down. Eddie must be panicking. I felt sorry for him. Our systems were not working. Could you imagine how that must feel? On your first day, during the first couple of hours on your new job, everything just stops and everyone is waiting on you to fix the problem. I hope he deals well with pressure. I looked up at the clock. It's 10:15. Since I couldn't get to my work, I decided that I would go to Eddie's office and see what the status was. I needed to know.

I was passing by the server room when I heard a voice that I didn't recognize. "Do you have any idea what you've done? In the future call me before you do anything. Oh man, I can't believe this. You have no idea how big of mistake it was to reset the configuration. I don't even know where to start. It's going to take me forever to fix this. This is just a mess."

"I did just what the tech support people told me to do. You've got to fix this, Jake. This can't be happening to me. Don't we have a backup or something? It can't take that long to restore a backup can it? We've got some sort of redundant system or something don't we? Come on Jake, give me an answer."

"Are you kidding me? I can't believe that you erased the configuration. Eddie!"

I heard Jerry's voice as he said, "That doesn't sound good, Eddie. Jake knows what he's doing. What are you going to do now Eddie?"

I could hear the anger and fear in his voice as I heard Eddie respond. "Shut up Jerry. I'll take care of this. I tried to call you Jake. All I got was your stupid voice mail. You're going to be making a lot of money helping me run this company and I need to be able to get in touch with you anytime I need you. I need a way to be able to page you. I couldn't get in touch with you and I had to do something. You don't understand. I've been getting calls from everybody in this building all morning. None of them can log in or get their work done. I'm just lucky that everyone in upper management except for Jim is gone. That gives us some time to fix this mess. I did the right thing Jake. I called tech support before I did anything. They're the ones that said to reset the configuration. It's not my fault. You would expect the tech support staff at the company that made this stuff could help."

"You can't rely on someone in tech support. Think about it Eddie. If that person in tech support had the kind of skills you just described, they wouldn't be working in tech support would they? Those folks in tech support are normally new staff members. They're reading a script and they have a database of potential combinations of problems and solutions. They don't know the specifics of your systems. They can't. They're getting trained at your expense. I'm not saying they don't try to help, but they don't know your systems or your level of expertise. They can only help so much. If, and when, you find someone in tech support that's good, write down their name and ask for them every time you call. They're still not going to be able to give you the best support. What you need for real support is someone who knows your systems, has had their hands on them, understands how you use them and knows something about your business. You need me buddy! Call me first. If you can't get in touch with me, just wait until you can. I won't let you down. I still can't believe you reset the configuration."

"I don't want to hear about the configuration. It's done. How long is it going to take to fix it? Can't we rig something so these folks can get some work done?"

"No, we can't rig something up! This has to done right. It could take days to fix this mess. This isn't like adding a new user, a printer or changing a password. We've got all weekend to get this fixed. Relax; we need to see the big picture here."

"What am I going to tell everybody? This is my first day in charge of this department. I can't let this happen. I'm not going to look like I don't know what I'm doing. What am I going to do?"

"Relax. This is going to work out. It's not like you to panic. Didn't you tell me that Craig was fired yesterday and that his entire crew quit?"

"Yes. They got the blame for the email problems and Craig blew up. That was the straw that broke Rick's back. He let Craig go. The rest of the IT staff just walked out."

"There's the answer to your problem Eddie. It's easy, tell them Craig or one of his staff left a virus or a bug in the system. Because of what they did, the network has to be shut down and reconfigured. No one here knows what that is or will ever know the difference. I'll back you up. I won't say that Craig or his staff actually caused this. That can easily be implied. I will say that a virus or a bomb caused these problems. Meanwhile, you better figure out a way to tell your people that this system won't be functional till Monday at the earliest. By the way, my weekend rates aren't cheap. You and I are going to run these systems for a long time buddy."

I could hear the smirk in Eddie's voice as he said, "That's good Jake, very good. We can turn this whole thing around. Everyone knows how mad Craig and his staff were about what happened. Everyone will believe that they messed up our systems. That's really good."

Jerry added, "This'll work. Nobody around here will have any trouble believing that Craig or some member of his staff did this. Everyone knows those guys could have caused us these kinds of problems. Everybody thinks they've been making a mess around here for a long time. You could end up being the hero, Eddie."

"We can put a spin on this and have everyone thinking you actually fixed the problem. It's great!"

"This is good! Prepare to watch the master at work. I need to make an announcement to the entire company. I'll have them eating out of my hand in no time."

I couldn't believe what I'd just heard. Everywhere I looked in this crazy house, I found more crazy things going on and more crazy people in charge. Eddie had been in charge of our IT department for less than 4 hours and he'd already crashed the entire system. Not only had he crashed the system but he was getting ready to lie to the entire company. These guys were about to embark on a doublespeak maneuver. You know where you convince everyone that black is white, inside out, upside down and chaos rules the world. Eddie was going to come out of this smelling like a rose. If I hadn't accidentally overheard this conversation, I would probably believe every word of the load of crap that these guys were about to feed everybody. I turned around and headed back to my office. I need to get out of here before the walls tumble down on top of these clowns.

Just as I sat down at my desk, I heard Eddie's voice over the office intercom.

"May I have your attention please? This is Eddie. For those of you that haven't heard, I'd like to let you know that I am now in charge of your IT department. Craig and the members of his staff are no longer with us. As many of you are already aware, our systems are currently experiencing severe difficulties due to an attack from a virus which was left in our systems. We have identified the virus as the source of our problems. We are working on restoring our systems as quickly as possible. Due to the severity of this attack, our systems will be down all weekend. By Monday afternoon we hope to have our systems restored to normal operations. If you have critical needs as to emails or other issues, please don't hesitate to stop by my office. Thank you for your understanding and your support. We'll get through this and we will do it together."

I was glad that I was sitting down. I couldn't believe that this was really happening. Why was I working here? I shouldn't say working here today because without my computer I couldn't get a lot of my work done. I guess I could call some of my clients on the phone. What would I say to them? Guess what's going on in the crazy house? You won't believe this one. OK I'll stop. I need to stay out of these issues. They're none of my business. I have to understand that I don't have any control over what goes on around here. I just work here. I'll try to focus on something positive. Lunch. That's positive. I'll call someone and go have lunch. I picked up the phone and made a lunch date with a friend of mine. She doesn't work here, or know anything about this place and that will help me forget about the mess at least for a little while.

Lunch was great and it had the intended effect. As I drove back to the office I was actually making an effort to review, regroup and determine what I could get done at work this afternoon. I knew that I wouldn't have a computer so I wouldn't be able to get a lot of things done. Jerry had some samples and with his help I could get some of them out to my clients. I could place a few calls to my clients and discuss some outstanding issues. After that, I would still be able to get out early and get ready to enjoy the weekend with my friends. I had a plan and it's a good one for me.

I passed Jerry as I walked down the hall. He said, "Can you believe what Craig and those guys did to our systems? We're lucky that Eddie is taking care of things."

Instead of voicing what I really believed, I remembered that there are things around here that I will never change and that I'll be gone from here soon, so I simply said, "I can't believe it, none of it. Is there any chance that we might get back up today?" As I asked the question I thought to myself these guys work together like some sort of political "SPIN" machine. I wish they would offer that kind of effort when we're trying to make things actually work around here.

"I don't think so. If anyone can get this mess straightened out, Eddie will. He says it will be running Monday afternoon. There ought to be some way the company could recover the damages that Craig and his staff have caused. Maybe Rick can take it out of their severance package."

"I don't know about that. I just want to be able to get my work done."

I thought to myself, I can't go there, Jerry. I know what you guys are pulling. I won't help you stir up another lynch mob. I've already seen what lynch mobs can do around here. Don't expect me to help you blame someone else and don't you dare ask me to help you take something away from them. They already lost their jobs!! I've got to stop thinking about this. I'm just going to get upset. I need to get away from Jerry and focus on other things so I said, "I've got to get back to my office. I've got a phone call coming in from a client."

"I was just heading out for lunch. Can I bring you anything?"

"No, I just had lunch. I do need to get some of those samples from you sometime this afternoon. I really need to send them out before I leave today."

"Let's go to my office and take care of that right now."

"I've got to catch that phone call in my office first. It should take me about 15 minutes. I'll come to your office as soon as I get done."

"I'll be waiting in my office"

The phone was ringing as I walked into my office. It wasn't the business phone call that I had been expecting. It was my friends that I was expecting for the weekend. Their flights had come in early and they wanted to surprise me. They had done just that. They were here at the front desk right now, waiting for me to come and get them. Talk about timing. I felt one of those smiles that come from deep inside your heart begin to leap right out of my chest. It was all I could do to resist running down the hall as I headed out to get my friends.

When I saw them we all ran together, hugged and laughed. It felt so good. I didn't realize how much I needed a hug and a laugh. As we walked back to my office, we started to talk and catch up on each other's lives. One of my friends said, "This place looks really nice. Everything looks new, the building looks great, and it looks like you're doing well."

"If you had asked me six months ago I would have told you everything was great. So many crazy things have gone wrong around here since then I just can't say that I like it here anymore."

"Well you still look like you're happy. You look great."

"Thanks. It's so great to see you guys. You all look great. I'm OK. This isn't the type of place that I feel like I can build a future in anymore. I need to get out of here as soon as I can. Listen, I have to stop by Jerry's office and get some samples to send to a client. As soon as I package those, send them out, call my client and let them know they're on the way we can get out of here."

"We can help you wrap them up. Isn't Jerry the creep you told us about that stares at your chest the entire time he talks to you?"

"That's him. You've all been properly warned."

As we headed into Jerry's office, he had a smile that looked like he had just won the lottery. He jumped to his feet and said, "Jane, you didn't tell me how absolutely beautiful your friends were. Ladies, my name is Jerry and it's my pleasure to meet you."

"Reel yourself in Jerry or I'll call your wife and have her pop that leash again. These ladies are way out of your league. I'm here to get the samples. Where are they?"

"Easy girl. Let your friends speak for themselves. The samples are over there in those briefcases. Take whatever you need. I'll try to entertain your guests."

I hurried and collected the samples I needed. I knew the standards that my friends had when it came to being entertained and they weren't drunk enough to find Jerry anywhere near meeting those standards. As a matter of fact they were sober and smart enough to cut him off at the knees. If I hadn't been in a hurry to get out of there, it might have been fun to watch the show. My friends would have had Jerry begging for mercy in no time. As it was, I thanked Jerry for the samples and we all headed towards my office.

Back in my office my friends and I continued to catch up on each other's lives as I sorted and packaged the samples for my client. It was nice to focus on something good. I was just beginning to enjoy our conversation when we were interrupted. When I looked up I saw Jerry, Eddie and some guy I didn't know walking through the doorway to my office. Their eyes were all running all over my friends like prison searchlights. It would have been embarrassing for them if they had the class to be embarrassed. As the drool began to drip from their lips I said, "Can I help you guys?"

Looking at my friends as he spoke to me Eddie replied, "I didn't know we would be interrupting anything. We just needed to check something on your computer."

These guys were definitely here to check something out. My friends and I knew very well what the three stooges wanted to check out. That idiot Jerry had broken his neck to tell these fools that my friends were here. These guys weren't too obvious.

"What do you need to check out? Maybe I can help."

"Thanks but we'll take care of it. I think it's an ID10T Error. Do you know Jake?'

I thought to myself, I know he's part of the scam you're running on this entire company. I haven't met him but I've sure heard him talk. I remember he talks about things like, "There's the answer to your problem. Craig or one of staff left a virus or a bug in the system, no one will ever know the difference, I'll back you up and you and I are going to run these systems for a long time." I haven't met Jake but I think I know a bit about his character. He's a liar and a jerk.

"Jane. Have you met Jake?"

I was holding back the anger I felt as I said, "No, I haven't. Hello Jake."

Jake held out his hand and responded, "It's certainly my pleasure Jane. I've heard a lot of good things about your from Eddie and Jerry."

I wasn't about to shake this guys hand. "Nice to meet you. Sorry, my hands are full right now. Are you a new staff member?"

"No. I'm here to help Eddie work on your computer systems. I've got my own company."

Eddie added, "You'll be seeing Jake around here quite a bit. I've known him for a long time. We're lucky that he's got time to help us out. He's been kind enough to squeeze us into his busy schedule. He's doing me and our company a favor."

While Eddie was talking to me, Jerry and Jake were busy trying to get the attention of my friends. My friends were pros at shutting down unwanted attention. These clowns didn't have a chance. They were lucky that I didn't let my friends' toy with them.

"That's nice when somebody does you a favor isn't it Eddie? Speaking of a favor, I've got one to ask of you. I'm trying to finish up and get out of here early. As you can see my friends are already here so why don't you come back later to do whatever it is you need to do on my computer. I'll be gone and you can do whatever you need in here."

"Sure, I can come back later if that's what you would like. Aren't you going to introduce me to your friends?"

"I'm sorry. Girls, this is Eddie. He's in charge of our IT department."

Everyone said hello to Eddie and I finished putting the samples in the package.

"I need to make a phone call now. It's time for some privacy. You boys need to leave"

"I'll be finished in just a minute Jane."

"You can finish later Eddie. Take your crew and leave."

"You being awfully pushy"

"For some strange reason Eddie, you and your little helpers suddenly got an urgent need to work on a computer that you've already told me I can't use until Monday. I'm not stupid. You guys just wanted to meet my friends. Well, you've done that and now I need to finish what I'm doing so my friends and I can get out of here. I'm not being pushy Eddie. Thank you for your help. Now take your crew and leave so I can finish up and get out of here."

Eddie pouted like a teenager as he mumbled, "Nice to meet you ladies"

Jerry probably thought my friends were impressed with him because he still had that "I don't have clue" smile on his face when he said, "It's been my pleasure."

Jake just left without saying a word.

No sooner had the three stooges left my office than my friends and I broke out into uncontrollable laughter. It felt so good to laugh. It felt like freedom. These are my friends and I am going to have a great weekend. It's good to have friends. It will be good to get out of here.

ID10T Errors

---

1. Downtime.

Downtime must be considered as a security risk because it represents a threat to normal business operations and a huge potential cost to your organization. Simply put, system downtime means lost money. We can only guess that Eddie's exercise in the use of an unscheduled downtime for the entire computer systems was his way to emphasize the importance of maintaining a stable technical environment. We're sure he just wanted to demonstrate that technology could have an immediate and direct affect on the company's bottom line. I doubt that Eddie had the intention to shut down the entire system but the situation he created and the environment at this company made this sort of problem inevitable. Eddie's first day in charge of the department IT was truly a very expensive venture.

There wasn't any evidence of anyone with the ability to understand or to calculate the "cost of downtime" within our company. Eddie's cost to the company may never be realized. Rick and the folks in our company seemed to see no need to develop real business skills. They chose instead to rely on their parent companies far too much. Not having that luxury, most companies must have a plan to avoid downtime as much as possible and definitely need a full appreciation of just how expensive downtime can be.

Infrastructure technologies are a part of the core of normal business operations today. No longer can the IT department be considered as office automation or as a support unit within your business. As companies become more interdependent across business units and extend their supply chains, the need to maintain a stable technical environment is greater today than it has ever been. Downtime can impact the core business, related businesses, clients and customers all along the chain. Today, more than ever, IT department's performance will directly reflect on the total success of your business. In today's business environment it is imperative that you convey to your staff and others the importance of avoiding downtime and maintaining systems availability.

Every day, you and your employees depend more and more on computer systems in order to do your jobs. Downtime, such as that evidenced in our story, can mean potential lost sales, stoppages in communications and disruptions for normal business operations. Jane was unable to finish her presentation, Jim couldn't get to his accounting records, Connie was unable to do her job and poor Jerry wasn't able to do whatever poor Jerry does. Downtime costs to US businesses alone have been estimated at a cost of more than 5 billion dollars per year.

While Eddie gave us a great example of what "downtime" is, there are many different definitions of the term "downtime." Our definition is simple, the systems applications are available or they aren't. A system should be considered essentially "down" if system users cannot use the applications on that system. When you attempt to calculate the "cost of downtime", there may be a variance in the percentage of who or what it is that is affected, but I have found that this basic concept of availability is a good rule of thumb to follow.

A simple formula to calculate the "cost of downtime" COD might look like this:

COD = Hours of Downtime x (User Cost / Hour + Business Lost / Hour)

A formula such as the one above cannot offer you a complete or true "cost of downtime". There are so many other components and factors that must be considered in the equation. The following list of questions that you might find useful in your efforts to estimate the true "cost of downtime". The answers you find to these questions within you own organization will help you to better define, understand and estimate your true "cost of downtime".

- What are the components that could have an impact on your "cost of downtime"?
- What are the direct and indirect employee cost that are related to downtime?
- What are the employee and IT recovery cost related to downtime?
- What are the cost of expenses that would not be incurred if the systems were operating normally?
- What lost sales and/or services to clients were involved?
- What cost will you incur in your efforts to minimize these losses?

The following are examples of two different methods that could be used to determine the "cost of downtime" to an organization. This first example is based on a 1-hour downtime scenario. This small example clearly illustrates how quickly the true "cost of downtime" can escalate. Downtime has a direct path to your company's bottom line.

10 users that are completely down:	$ 250.00 (10 X $25/hr salary = $250)
100 users that have been 30 % affected:	$ 750.00 (100 X $25/hr X .30 = $750.00)
110 users 1 hour each to restore 110 users:	$2,750.00 (110 X $25 = $2,750.00)
3 IT staff to restore normal operations:	$ 180.00 (3 X $60 = $180.00)
Partial estimated cost of 1-hour downtime:	$3,930.00

The second example of estimating the true "cost of downtime" is to divide your company's gross annual revenue by your hours of operation. The resulting number will represent a dollar value per business hour for your system. Multiplying that dollar value per hour by the number of hours of downtime in the past year will show the cost of that downtime.

Gross annual revenue:	$ 1,000,000.00
Hours of operation:	2,100
Dollar value per business hour :	$ 476.19
Unscheduled downtime in hours:	72
"Cost of downtime"	$ 34,285.68

A true and complete reflection of a total "cost of downtime" would require more information than what is offered in our examples. Our intention by using these examples is to offer you a good starting point. The solution that works best for you in your efforts to find the true "cost of "downtime" will probably involve a combination of methods, formulas, exceptions and additions that are individual to you and your organization. You and your organization, and your ability to learn, implement, and manage the availability of your infrastructure and the associated technologies, will be directly reflected in your level of success. Those solutions, once found and implemented, will decrease unscheduled downtime, increase your company's productivity, build confidence and, of course, save your business large sums of money.

2. Lack of leadership.

Unfortunately the lack of leadership within this company has to be addressed again. It is at the very core of all of the problems and security risks that this fictional organization faces. The environment that exists within this company is one where the dangers of theft, fraud, corporate espionage and destructive staff members like Eddie thrive.

This company went through traumatic changes on Thursday as an entire department's staff left the company. At a critical time when the remaining staff needed to physically see and feel management's support, all of the upper management team, with the exception of Jim, vanished. They had left the building. They deserted their company. Once again, there was no leadership to be found. There was just a void.

I will state once again that I believe that most people want to work together and will do well if:

a. You let them know what the expectations are and where the boundaries are.
b. They know where you need help and where they can get help.
c. What the rewards are for compliance.
d. What the consequences are for violation.
e. You are consistent.

3. Outsourcing - control vs. cost.

Reasons why an organization might consider outsourcing:

1. The desire to obtain cost reductions.
2. Availability of additional staff (knowledge, skills)
3. The need for business flexibility or changing markets.
4. The requirements to mitigate business and technology risks.

Outsourcing is growing at double-digit rates. In any outsourcing engagement there is a normal trade-off of control vs. cost. That is one of the fundamental truths of outsourcing. The decision to outsource is normally based on a cost savings for less direct control. Eddie's decision to choose Jake as his local vendor for his company's outsourcing needs was not based on normal conditions. His lack of IT knowledge and the urgency of the downed systems were the driving forces behind his decision. He has placed a tremendous amount of faith in Jake to maintain the availability of his IT systems. Eddie has lost control of the outsourcing engagement and his systems. Eddie's lack of knowledge, the company's lack of structure and the overall lack of accountability have all combined to give Jake, the outsourcing vendor, almost total control. Eddie can't even effectively manage this situation. Companies that fail to lead and effectively manage all aspects of an outsourcing relationship will spend more money than is necessary, obtain fewer benefits, will not achieve their desired goals and could potentially threaten the long term success of the organization itself. Eddie and Jake have also shown us that their involvement alone exposes our company to the additional risk of theft, fraud, corporate espionage and much more. Jane was correct in her perception that these conditions were full of all kind of dangers.

Jake mentioned that Eddie had erased the configuration and that it would take all weekend to repair and restore the systems to normal operations. That may or may not be the case. With the limited information we have been given in our story, we're not sure whether the configuration referred to was the CMOS configuration on a server which would take less than 20 minutes to reset or whether it was the configuration on firewalls and routers which could take considerably longer to repair. There is no one left with the expertise to verify how long the repairs should take, cost or what the real issues are. Eddie has definitely lost control of the entire outsourcing engagement and its cost. He can only hope that he can trust Jake and that no one in his organization has the knowledge or ability to check into his IT department. As we have mentioned in earlier chapters, it is always good to keep your outsourcing relationships competitive.

Methods to create competitive events in your sourcing arrangement:

- Maintain the training of your internal staff to a level that would allow you to take over the project at any time.
- Do whatever is needed to prevent any one vendor from having a lock on your business.
- Competitively bid some services to keep pricing and terms realistic.
- Give other vendors the opportunity to learn about your needs and build their own knowledge base.

Outsourcing of key business processes, such as Information Technology, Engineering, Financial Analysts, Architects, Human Resources, Logistics and Shipping are increasingly becoming a standard practice for large companies. Our knowledge base, skills, processes, procedures, infrastructures and activities are being carved up and redistributed to other labor markets such as India, Philippines, China, Russia, Mexico and more. As you consider your own outsourcing needs and begin conducting your own cost/benefit analysis I would suggest that you consider both a short and long term approach. As you consider the normal trade-off of control vs. cost you should also consider the cost of redistribution and the risk of losing control.

5.   ROI – Return on investment.

When we talk of things such as technology or outsourcing we often talk about the potential ROI. An ROI is perceived as good when the expected benefits exceed the anticipated costs by enough margins to justify the risks. When performing such calculations it is best to be conservative in nature to insure more realistic results. In a Return on Investment (ROI) calculation, two values are required:

- The value to your organization (i.e. the "Return")

The focus should not only be on what is gained by the purchase or implementation, but what could be potentially be lost by not purchasing or implementing.

- The cost to your organization (i.e. the "Investment")

Missing any of the related costs will result in an error in ROI calculation.

It is true that we need look no further than the bottom line (Profitability) to find the short-term success or failure of an organization. Long-term success however is a product of that same bottom line and things like leadership, teamwork, structure, accountability, value, trust, security, profitability and long-term investments. These are some of the basic components of a successful organization. The lack of any of these components constitutes a real security risk. Unfortunately our company has very few of the qualities needed for success. Bottom line, I'm glad I don't work there.

Summary

In this book we have presented the story of a fictional company as told from various staff members' perspectives. We have attempted to deal with a wide variety issues and problems. For those of you that have read our story and felt like some of the issues didn't get resolved, you're right, they didn't. We didn't mean to leave you hanging. Since we do not know the specifics of your environment and the conditions that you work and live in we have not attempted to publish a "how to, step by step, guide". We have taken a more realistic approach. An example of this would be Jerry (the salesman) and his problems with his company credit card. We didn't have those issues resolved, as in real life those issues would take days or even weeks to resolve. What we did was to offer some guidelines and suggestions. For those suggestions to have any chance of working for you they need to tempered with the specifics of the environment and conditions that you work and live in. Our intent is to better serve you.

It is our hope that you have found this book entertaining, informative and helpful. This book is part the ID10T Errors series of publications. Subjects such as identity theft, hackers' diary, project management, outsourcing, management, supply chain, ERP, forecasting, consulting and surviving the corporate culture are just some of the areas that our future publications will address. The style of this particular book is a sample of the wide variety of authors, subjects and styles you will have to choose from when you're reading and enjoying any of the ID10T Errors publications.

Thank you for choosing one of our publications. Please be aware that our series of publications is ongoing and always in search of new authors and ideas. If you are an author that would like your book to be a part of our series or have an idea for a publication please contact us at:

Attn: Rick Smith
Subject: Ideas
ID10T Errors, Inc.
P.O. Box 6037
Hickory, NC 28603
Email: ideas@id10terrors.com

Acknowledgements

I would like to thank my wife, Becky Frye-Smith and our children (Brooke and Gaither) for all of the love and support I have received from them. My wife has supported my efforts and understood my resolve.

I would also like to thank my mother, sister, her husband, their children and my entire family for the love and support I have and continue to receive from all of them.